When the Duke Comes to Play...

When the Duke Comes to Play...

Curves & Cravats

KELSEY SWANSON

This is a work of fiction. Names, characters, places, and incidents are products of the author's imagination or are used fictitiously and are not to be construed as real. Any resemblance to actual events, locales, organizations, or persons, living or dead, is entirely coincidental.

Cover Design by Holly Perret, The Swoonies Romance Art

ISBN: 979-8-89283-122-2

For curvy women everywhere.

Prologue

London, 1825

What had she been thinking?

Ariel Tilbury paced back and forth in the front parlor of the Mayfair Townhouse she shared with her elder brother, Arnold. It had been just the two of them since their father's death three years prior and, with Arnold out for the evening enjoying fully the perks of being a male with a title, she was alone. The silence of the house was unfamiliar and heavy, fraught with anticipation.

Or was it, perhaps, judgment?

She twisted her fingers until the knuckles blanched and then glanced for easily the forty-third time between the carefully drawn drapes and the clock upon the mantle.

Two hours and twenty-nine minutes remained until the clock chimed to announce her thirtieth birthday.

And one agonizingly long minute until her guest arrived.

She had been so confident one month prior when the idea had first occurred to her.

She'd bubbled over with nervous excitement when, just three days earlier, she'd decided to follow through and discreetly requested her friend contact the agency.

Then, she'd woken that morning to a jittery feeling in her limbs, as if she was physically unable to sit still and wait for the hours to pass by with all the speed of hot, caramelized sugar dripping from a spoon.

Now that the hour was upon her, however, Ariel was regretting her bravado, cursing her brilliantly awful, scandalous idea, and contemplating hiding beneath her covers and pretending she hadn't heard the knock on the door when it finally did come.

She was miserably anxious, practically crawling out of her skin with each passing second. She regretted everything about the situation—her harebrained idea, being born that sunny day three decades prior, every experience and choice that had led her to this moment…

She'd just fisted her hands in her skirts, having concluded that she would cancel all of it—forget the sum of money she had already paid and retreat to her room—when a knock finally sounded upon the door.

An ice-blue wave of shock jolted through Ariel's body, freezing her limbs and stalling her breath. She didn't know how long she stood there frozen, but it was long enough that the caller rapped against the door once more, slightly louder and more impatient than the first time.

It served to prod her into motion. She could have been a coward and remained silent until the knocker retreated, but that was not in her nature.

Stiffly, she moved one halting foot and then the other until she somehow wound up in the entryway, facing the door to her future. She raised a trembling hand to the knob and turned it while holding the air in her lungs for buoyancy.

What had ever possessed her to hire a male courtesan *for the* evening?

Chapter One

It was a time-honored state of being that Society was unkind to those who did not fit in; especially females.

A woman who focused too much on her family was antisocial, possibly viewing herself as too good for Society. A woman who spent too much time on charitable endeavors was generating a saintly facade; holier-than-thou. A woman who dressed too fashionably was either vain or trying much too hard. A woman who didn't dress well enough was frumpy and unappealing. A woman who danced too much was loose with her morals and her favors; a woman who danced too little was a wallflower. Decline too many proposals—whatever the reason may be—and you were a tease or snobbish; receive no proposals and you were pitied as being in dire danger of becoming a spinster, dusty and set firmly upon the shelf.

Perhaps the greatest of sins were the ones difficult or impossible to change—the physical ones or those who made a woman who she was at the very core of her being.

Women too tall, too intelligent, too outspoken, too shy, too pock-marked, too sallow, too freckled, too plump…these were the women who suffered the most for no reason other than something about them was deemed different.

Lady Ariel, sister to Arnold Francis Martin Tilbury, Earl of Darby, was one woman unfortunate enough to be in possession of several of the aforementioned "undesirable" traits.

At just shy of six feet in height thanks to sturdy Northern ancestry, she towered over many men in Society.

Having received the same education as her elder brother and gone on to cultivate her extensive library, she was often more intelligent than those same men; though she'd learned early on that they were not fond in the least of being reminded of this fact.

At twenty-nine years and three-hundred-and-sixty-four days in age with not a single proposal to her name above a septuagenarian baron looking for his third wife, she was unquestionably a spinster in need of a good dusting.

She'd removed her bonnet a few too many times when she'd snuck off to the gardens to read, so a healthy smattering of freckles was splashed across her nose and the round apples of her cheeks.

And her figure was well past the "pleasantly plump" side of the *ton*'s scale. To state it plainly, she was fat. Or so she's been told, both behind her back and to her face more times than she could count at that point.

At first, this had crushed her as it would anyone receiving such venomous barbs. Words can be crushing to a girl who wanted nothing more than to be accepted and welcomed into the glittering world she'd read of and heard so much about. The reality of the darkness flitting just beneath the bejeweled surface was enough to make her wish she'd never left her library.

As time went on, however, Ariel had come to appreciate the sturdiness of her body, the luscious curves she firmly believed lent a more feminine air to her tall frame. She enjoyed long walks at an aggressive pace, so her stamina was undoubtedly greater than many titled ladies who grew winded from walking up too many stairs, or faint from lack of sustenance so they could fit into one special gown or another, shamed into their willowy grace and delicate paleness by generations of ladies who came before them. Ariel didn't know if it was because she'd never known her mother or any other female figure of consequence in her life, but she simply hadn't experienced the same pressures at home. Instead, she did as her brother did. She ate what she loved, she appreciated good brandy, she could curse as fluently as any man, and she'd developed a thick skin.

Well, as thick a skin as a woman who has been passed over, mocked, and sneered at for most of her life.

Ariel had gradually learned to tell herself that there wasn't much she could do about any of it. She couldn't influence the minds and ingrained opinions of others, and there was little she could do about herself without losing those things she loved most about who she was. She'd inherited the same sturdy build as her brother, but she had the unfortunate circumstance of having been born with breasts instead of bollocks. Men seemed to appreciate her ample bosom well enough (if the tilt of their lascivious gazes was any indication), but it seemed like the rest of her lagged well behind in their estimation.

Weary of being overlooked, looked through, and blatantly ignored, she had finally decided to handle her frustration on her own and take matters into her own hands.

The women in her close circle were all married ladies and many were also mothers, each of them happy enough to discuss marital matters (the joys of sharing a bed with a man, for one…). What had begun as murmurs and whispered titters between the few ladies recently wed had spread to encompass every woman of their group until Ariel was the only one left out. Luckily for her, she was allowed in on the conversations when she reached the ripe old age of five and twenty. She was gradually allowed in on these hallowed secrets, of climaxes and naughty adventures, of forbidden words like "cunny" and "cock", of rapturous embraces and kisses that left a woman breathless. Of course, she'd listened and been utterly enthralled, but she also had no point of reference for these conversations. Many of these descriptions eluded her and were beyond her sheltered mind's comprehension. She hadn't made it nearly thirty years of life without curiously exploring her own body alone in the dark, testing secret places with tentative fingers, but she always lost her nerve and shied away when the sensations grew too overwhelming.

But no longer.

Ariel was fed up with living vicariously through others. She was tired of having nothing to contribute to her friends' deliciously naughty conversations. And she was finished with not understanding everything they discussed.

She didn't know where the idea had come from or when it had first occurred, but once the first tendril took root in her mind, it had spread rapidly like ripe strawberry plants; creeping and taking hold, impossible to uproot or completely eradicate, bearing fruit despite little care or mindfulness until it became impossible to ignore.

She'd bolstered her courage, steeled her nerves, and requested a recommendation from a dear friend with knowledge of the illicit industry. A missive had been sent to the exclusive establishment and the meeting was arranged with the utmost discretion.

Men in his profession went under any number of titles, but the fact of the matter was a male prostitute was scheduled to arrive at Ariel's home by half-nine the evening before her thirtieth birthday.

As wracked with nerves as she was, Ariel refused to spend another birthday pathetic and untouched, wondering what it would feel like to experience physical affection. She planned on performing the transaction, educating herself, and moving on with her life more worldly and more confidently than before. Even if she never married or had a family, at least she would have this night.

Now, with said caller knocking on her door, however, she was reconsidering the entire scenario.

She should have donned another persona, used a false name, and *not* given out her address… But she couldn't very well have rented a room at a hotel on her own (for one, she was a woman, and, two, that gossip would travel swifter than a plague) and, while she'd wracked her brain for other options for location, she'd come up short.

Though Arnold was evasive about his schedule, she knew full well her brother was spending the evening with his mistress and he never returned home until the wee hours of the following morning. She'd told their elderly, nearly deaf butler to retire early for the night and their housekeeper was off visiting her sister for two days of leave. Two of their maids had a room above the mews behind their home. And Ariel was as alone as she could be.

There was another rap on the front door and the thumps vibrated through the brass knob and up her arm, jolting every nerve into awareness.

Just before she turned the knob, Ariel was struck by a recollection: She was quite certain she had sent instructions to knock at the back door so none wandering the streets or heading to other outings witnessed the man's arrival. It would most certainly not do if anyone asked questions or reported back to her brother, but she supposed it was too late to worry about that now. He was already there. She held her breath and pulled on the door.

She didn't know what she'd expected from a fancy man—a working male hired for the feminine pleasure of the most carnal forms— but it wasn't quite the dashing figure before her. He was tall; at least a handful of inches above her, so it was an interesting change where she had to look up into his face.

To speak of his face…it was hewn of marble. More angular, elegant lines she had never seen, even in the most beautiful male Grecian sculptures in the museum. There was a small cleft in his chin, but it served only to accentuate the sharpness of his jaw and the fullness of his lower lip. His aquiline nose led up to bold, straight slashes of dark brows that hovered above the most enchanting eyes caught somewhere between blue and steely gray. Beneath the sharp brim of his beaver hat, she could see a hint of deep brown curls. His body was mostly disguised by the voluminous fabric of a black greatcoat and, while the garment was usually designed for warmth and to exaggerate the width of the male shoulders, she sincerely doubted exquisite tailoring could create the magic standing before her. That was all God.

One of those dashing brows rose as the mesmerizing eyes focused on her and it took her a moment to realize why that was. It wasn't the done thing for a lady to answer the door herself.

Then again, it also wasn't the done thing for an unmarried lady to hire a male courtesan to visit her at her brother's home and deflower her.

To his credit, he did not comment on any of it; instead, his gaze swept her from head to toe. "I have an appointment," he said, and the surprisingly deep tone of his voice threw vibrations throughout her body, shook her so deeply that it took her several heartbeats to find her voice.

"Y—Yes. Do come in." She stepped to the side; the man hesitated only one moment more before brushing past her. She poked her head through the doorway, her eyes darting about to survey the empty street before she ducked back inside.

She found the man's captivating gaze assessing her with an unexpected intensity. He'd removed his hat to reveal to her that he did, indeed, have some of the most lusciously curly hair that she'd ever beheld. It was boyish and innocent, standing incongruently with the rest of his smoldering looks. She absently wondered if it was as soft as it appeared.

And then she realized she'd likely know by the end of the night.

The very thought set her cheeks ablaze and she was immensely grateful for the dim lighting left behind after the butler had doused most of the candles before retiring. She exhaled an uneven breath. How did one conduct such business? Even have a conversation? What were words, again?

"May I…take your coat for you? Your hat?" She'd never taken anyone's coat and hat for them—had never thought to be in such a position to do so—then again, she never thought she'd proposition a man for intercourse. So, there she was. This was her life now. In for a penny, in for a pound, or so the saying went.

He cleared his throat and, very slowly, handed her his hat and swung his coat from his shoulders.

My, but had she been correct about his body beneath the layers of his coat. She stared dumbly for several minutes at the width of his shoulders, the trimness of his waist, and the staggeringly strong length of his legs in his well-fitted breeches and tall, polished Hessians. He dressed remarkably well for a man who did…what he did for a living.

Still, despite the fine appearance of his dress, there was something dangerous about him. It had to be his eyes.

"Would you like my card?" His voice snapped her back to attention and, belatedly, she realized she was holding his outer garments and had no idea what to do with them.

"No, that will not be necessary. I know just who you are." Had she been less nervous, she might have pondered the oddity of the inquiry, but she wasn't and she hadn't. How fancy must a fancy man be to have calling cards?

She nearly snorted aloud but caught herself just in time. It was probably bad form to laugh at one's silent jokes in such a situation.

"Are you alone?" the man asked, looking around as if more people would pop from the floral-papered walls. His voice was unexpectedly melodious.

"No; I mean, mostly." He stared at her in silence. "Our butler is quite old. And deaf. He's retired for the evening. He shouldn't interrupt anything." One of those dark brows quirked up at her again. Still, the silence stretched.

"Well," Ariel began awkwardly, still carrying the man's hat and cloak for lack of any appropriate place to hang them and not quite sure what to do with them; "I suppose we should begin. If you'll just…follow me, please." She began to lead the way back into the parlor—she wasn't quite ready to drag the man to her bedchamber just yet—when she miscalculated just how much fabric made up the greatcoat in her arms. The toe of her slipper hooked in a fold of the dark wool and she stumbled forward. She probably would have landed face-first in a pile on the floor had the man not caught her elbow with all the speed and grace of a kingfisher.

"Steady," he cautioned her.

"Oh!" Ariel righted herself and looked up into his face, having just realized why she found his voice so different. "Are you American?"

There was a wry tilt to his lips as if he were asked this often or it was commonly remarked upon. "I am."

"Interesting," she replied with a smile. This humanized the man, somehow; made him less intimidating now that she was aware of this single fact about him.

"Is it?" He made sure she found her feet once more before he released her.

She lifted a shoulder in response. "I suppose it makes you rather unique. I've never met an American before; let alone a man like you."

"Like me?"

Ariel's cheeks burned and she cleared her throat. "If you'll follow me, please?" She hiked the greatcoat higher in her arms and led the way. She glanced around in indecision before finally settling on draping the coat on a chair and resting the hat on top. The man eyed her decision, but, thankfully, did not remark upon the unorthodox behavior.

She watched as he proceeded to take a turn around the room with slow strides, examining the artwork and appraising the furniture. It didn't take long, not with the length of those legs of his. He seemed disinclined to speak, so she clenched her hands, steeled her spine, and broke the silence.

"I'm afraid I have never performed one of these transactions."

"No?" He faced her with his arms crossed behind his back; a single thick curl of hair fell across the middle of his forehead. He was somehow even more beautiful in the candlelight filling the parlor. His skin had a healthy glow to it as if he spent a great deal of time outdoors. She could now fully appreciate the sculpture of his face and the fine lines of his cheekbones. "I was under the impression that a great many women performed transactions such as this." Was that sarcasm? Wryness? A jaded personality? She decided it was probably some of all of it, likely inherent with the trade and the lifestyle.

"Really?"

He stared her down with those penetrating eyes of his. They flickered with intelligence and, perhaps, a measure of amusement. She chose to take it as a compliment.

She gave herself a mental shake, cleared her throat, and, on impulse, she gave him leave him to call her by her given name. "You may address me as Ariel." She was pleased with the steadiness and confidence her voice conveyed. It was not a liberty she'd ever offered a man and, for such a little thing, it was surprisingly thrilling. "It might feel strange to conduct such business with a wall of formalities between us."

The man examined her for several heavy seconds before replying. "Why, exactly, do you believe I am here, *Ariel*?" Her given name on his lips made her knees tremble. There was something so deliciously wicked about the casualness of it. She was alone with a man—a very handsome one, at that—for the first time in her life and he was using her name. If she overlooked the fact that she was paying him to do so, it was quite nice. And unbelievably exciting.

She exhaled a slow breath and spoke as evenly as she could. "Tomorrow I celebrate my thirtieth birthday. As I am sure you can see, I'm no conventional beauty. I'm fine with it; really, I am. I love myself, but men of the *ton* do not seem to agree. I have gone nearly three decades without a husband, an acceptable proposal, a decent suitor, or even a proper kiss. You, sir, have been hired because I have decided to take my life and my future into my own hands. I refuse to allow Society to dictate my life any longer, and I see no point in saving my virtue for a man who certainly does not exist. If I am to be a spinster for the rest of my days, then I do not wish to be an ignorant one. This is where you come in…" She held out her hands palms up, her voice as steady and as brave as she could make it. "I am a virgin, and I no longer wish to be one when the sun rises tomorrow."

Chapter Two

Charles nearly choked on his tongue.

Had the girl truly said what he thought she had?

He'd sensed something was off when the door was answered by a woman who—given her mein, carriage, and dress—was of obvious quality.

When she, herself, took his greatcoat and his hat and was then lost with what to do with them.

When he'd had an appointment to discuss the purchase of a damned horse from the Earl of Darby and had, instead, encountered only this woman. (Don't misunderstand him, she was an intriguing, attractive woman, but she was hardly the Earl of Darby.)

And this night was quickly turning into the strangest since he'd been tracked down at his firm in Boston and been informed that, due to a comedy of errors and an accident of birth, he was the new Duke of Ryton following the death of an elderly third cousin whom he'd never met.

While most of London had been abuzz since his reluctant arrival to claim his birthright, and he'd been dragged this way and that by everyone clamoring to gain an introduction to or host him at one event or another, this woman had most assuredly not been at any of those events.

For one, he liked to think she would have recognized him.

For another, he definitely would have remembered *her*.

She described herself as undesirable, but she was far from it in his eyes. Her tall, buxom figure was more than enticing; her curves begged to be gripped and molded to his body. She was a woman who could take everything he had.

She was not in her first bloom of youth, but that only drew him in further. He knew instantly that other men were intimidated by her; it was the only explanation he could come up with for why she hadn't been snapped up yet.

What a shame.

For them.

And an unexpected gift for *him*.

For that is what she was; a gift. And it appeared she intended to throw away what was viewed as the most precious asset a woman possessed because the strutting peacocks, fops, and dandies of London had no idea what stood before them. And Charles absolutely couldn't allow that to happen.

The dark pools of her eyes remained unwavering on his face. She held herself motionless. And he realized he needed to respond quickly, lest she come to the wrong conclusion.

His mind whirled in a way it never had before. Somehow, this situation was more confusing, more important than any other he'd made in his life. He felt as if more than just a woman's virtue rested upon his shoulders.

Perhaps her future.

Both their futures.

He was scheduled to spend very little additional time in London beyond that night. He'd only arrived the month prior at the solicitors' insistence to handle matters in person, apply his signature to necessary documents, and view a few properties he was determined to unload for sale at the earliest opportunity; it was clear from even the basic reports he'd received that they were of no benefit. The old duke had left things in fair enough shape. With the death tax paid and his identity confirmed, the duchy was firmly in his hold and Charles planned to leave for America within the fortnight with no near plans to return to this narrow little island. He had a life in Boston, and that life would continue whether or not he had the title of "Duke of Ryton" attached to his name. He would leave England in his wake and forget the grey and drizzly land and its stuffy people.

And then, his current predicament became immaculately clear to him like a bolt of lightning across an inky sky.

It took an embarrassingly short amount of time to convince himself that it was better that he do this horrible, reprehensible thing to save this woman—Ariel—from a fate far worse at the hands of some pox-ridden man who would be just as likely to leave her with a venereal disease as a thoughtless pregnancy. She had indicated that her brother wouldn't be home anytime soon—so much for polite Brits who kept appointments—and he could do her this service of divesting her of her maidenhead and take his leave before her brother returned. It felt twisted to view himself as being the benevolent one when, in reality, this would be no hardship whatsoever.

And then he would quit the country.

He truly didn't need to purchase the horse from Ariel's brother; quality horseflesh could certainly be found elsewhere. And he'd been planning to leave shortly anyway. He could give her this one night and they'd never lay eyes upon one another again. She'd never be the wiser for it either.

Charles closed the gap between them and took her hands in his, bringing them to his lips. She wore no gloves and the skin of her knuckles was soft against his lips and smelled faintly of night-blooming jasmine.

"My lady," he began, lowering his voice to a purr; "it would be my honor."

Ariel was quite certain she stopped breathing when the man spoke. And quite terrified she would never remember how to do so, so long as he continued to touch her. That would make the rest of this evening quite difficult, wouldn't it?

Oh my...

This was the man who would see her unclothed. He would touch her bare flesh. This beautiful man.

She was barely able to swallow past the lump in her throat.

And she would get to see all of him in return.

Her cheeks began to burn from within as if someone had lit a kiln beneath her skin.

Oh my...

"Lead the way, if you will, my lady." His murmur was low as he tilted his square chin to the door.

Right. She had to show him the way to her bedchamber. Ariel opened her mouth to speak, but no sound came out. She attempted to mask it by lowering her face and turning away. To her surprise, the man never let go of her. He intertwined their fingers as he trailed behind her. Never releasing her as she awkwardly led the way up the sweeping main staircase, past the judgmental painted expressions of ancestors whose eyes she knew she'd never again be able to meet after that night's debauchery, and down the dim hallway where the family bedchambers were located.

She had known the man less than a quarter of an hour, yet there was something bolstering about the surety of his grip, the large palm and long fingers. It was absurd, but Ariel was almost comforted by it.

The man had comforting hands.

They were sturdy hands in which a woman could be confident in placing herself.

Perhaps this was a good thing, given the unconventionality of their circumstances. It was nearly painful to remind herself that it was likely all an act anyway… This was a man who knew how to treat a woman—he made a living from it.

Ariel held her breath and opened the door to her bedchamber.

A sconce remained lit, casting a small orb of golden light in the dim room.

The man followed her in and pressed the door closed behind them. The silence was so heavy she swore he could hear her heartbeat as loud as a drum.

They stood there, staring, sizing one another up for what felt like an eternity before he spoke. "You needn't do this, Ariel." His words were quiet and he held himself unnaturally still. She might have believed him to be a shadow if it were not for the flash of his eyes and the glimmer of white teeth.

What he didn't understand was that she *did*. She did need to do this. She needed to know what it felt like, even just once. She wanted to feel desired and experience passion. It wasn't as if she was going to wear a sign broadcasting what she'd done for all to see. This was purely for her edification; for her to file away for however many decades of spinsterhood she had remaining. It was a lot of weight to place upon the shoulders of a strange man, but he was a professional.

"I must—I *want* to," she whispered and he inclined his head after a slight hesitation.

"If I do anything you do not desire—anything that does not bring you the utmost pleasure—you *must* tell me. It is the *only* rule."

Ariel bit the inside of her cheek so hard it made her eyes water; her knees practically buckled. She nodded in agreement.

"It is my job to give you nothing but pleasure, Ariel." He closed the gap between them, watching her all the while as if she were a hare who might bolt into the tall grass until he stood close enough that the toes of his boots brushed the hem of her skirts.

It was so novel to look up into a man's face; her unnatural height often left most men of the *ton* at a disadvantage when speaking to her. It made Ariel feel unexpectedly feminine…and excited.

She was engulfed in his masculine scent of starch, a hint of a woodsiness, and the musk of male skin. His hands skimmed up her arms; one paused at her shoulder and the other cupped the back of her head. A shiver skittered up and down her spine. "Have you been kissed before, Ariel?" It was of the utmost foolishness given their situation, but she was quickly becoming enamored of the way he said her name with his American accent—harder and more forceful, a manner uniquely his.

"No," she breathed. Her eyes flew to the elegant lines of his mouth, now tilting charmingly up at the corners.

"Perfect."

His head began to descend, her eyes fluttered closed, and then a thought struck her just before his lips touched hers. Her eyes flew open once more and one of her hands closed around his—very firm, very sizeable—forearm.

"Wait!"

To his credit, he froze so successfully that she wasn't sure he still lived.

"W—What is your name?" He didn't make her explain why she needed to know; she didn't need to mortify herself by admitting that it didn't feel right to receive her first kiss from a man whose name she did not know.

Instead, he simply answered her: "Charles."

"Thank you, Charles." She closed the small space between their lips and took her first kiss from a man.

Her first thought was how soft his lips were.

Her second was that, while this was nice and it was thrilling to be kissed, she was disappointed that this was all there was to it. The experience seemed rather incongruous with everything her friends had described. She hoped the rest of the evening was more in line with her expect—

"Here," the man called Charles murmured kindly against her mouth. She might have mistaken the sound of a smile in his tone… His other hand reached up and he cupped her face gently and tilted it ever so slightly before slanting his mouth over hers in a vastly different way. And his lips moved.

Oh yes, this was better.

She nearly jumped when she felt the tip of his tongue trace the seam of her lips. By all accounts, it should have been repulsive…instead, she sighed and allowed him access. She parted her lips and kissed him back, meeting the slow attack and retreat of his lips and tongue. He patiently demonstrated the rhythm, slowing her down when she would have been too eager in her ignorance. She must have been doing something right because a low growl rumbled up from deep in his throat like the rush of a tide when she touched her tongue to his.

He tasted of something sweet and smoky. The only word that came to mind was cherrywood—seductively rich and warm and comforting.

All at once, she became aware that the length of her body was pressed to his. She wasn't sure which of them had closed the gap between them, but she was well past the point of questioning the situation, wasn't she? What mattered was that every inch of the front of her was touching every inch of the front of him. Her breasts were pressed to the hard wall of his chest. One of his giant palms cupped the ample curve of her hip; his thumb caressed her through the fabric of her dress on its way to wrap around her waist. An expertly placed thumb canted her head back, allowing him to deepen the kiss, to devour her. Ariel's legs began to tremble and she was practically propped up by the impressive strength of his arms; what was more, she had no fear of falling.

Lest she melt completely, she twisted her fingers in the lapels of his jacket. Absently, she wondered at the fineness of the fabric and stitching, of the patterned silk waistcoat pressed flush with her breasts, but all thoughts were dashed away as his hand drifted from her chin to the throbbing pulse in her throat, to the soft skin of her collarbone, and the deep crevasse of her décolletage.

The graze of a fingertip traced the line of her cleavage, down to the neckline of her gown, drew a lazy pattern on the swell of her ample breast. The circles grew smaller as he neared the budding peak of her nipple.

"Are you well?" Charles asked, sounding almost pained. All capabilities of speech had fled her at that point and Ariel could only nod. She wasn't sure how well she was, she just knew she didn't want him to stop. The things he was doing made her skin unbearably hot. Every sweep of his tongue made her long to pull him closer until they were one. She whimpered when he nibbled her lower lip, so strong was the crashing wave of desire as it spread throughout her like fire catching the parched grasses at the end of a hot summer. She was kindling beneath his touch, primed and ready to ignite.

She nearly jumped out of her skin when the pad of his finger rasped against her erect, aching nipple through the silk of her dress. A gasp was ripped from her throat and she unwillingly tore her mouth from his as his large palm cupped the ample weight of her breast. Testing it. Savoring it. Kneading it with infinite reverence. Though she was untried, her body seemed to know what to do and it arched her into his touch. She subconsciously begged for more. She wanted to feel him tweak her nipple with nothing between them—to pluck the taut thread of desire strung through her body until she vibrated with it like a harp.

"Mmmm," he purred, his baritone voice further melting her. "You are sensitive here, aren't you? She caught half a glimpse of a wicked smile before he ducked his head and elicited another gasp from her throat. "I am very much going to enjoy this."

All thoughts fled her mind like a bird from a window when Charles replaced his fingers with his mouth, sucking, nibbling, and laving her with the flat of his tongue. The wetness soaking through the fabric of her bodice and underthings only heightened the sensations unleashed within her.

Ariel's hands flew to his head, pressing him closer, burying his face against her, and she learned that his hair was, indeed, even softer than it appeared. She relished the curls winding about her fingers, thrilled when he emitted a tiny moan after she gave the locks an experimental tug, nearly giddy when he demonstrated an unexpected amount of strength as he dipped and wrapped his arms beneath her bottom, standing and then slinging her over his shoulder.

"Oh! Oh, please don't!" Ariel was briefly mortified as she braced her palms on the broad plane of his back…until she realized he wasn't struggling against her weight in the least.

"Surely you cannot fault me for my eagerness," Charles replied lightly as he strode to her bed and dropped her gently to the thick mattress. "Not when your touch is so exciting." His smoldering eyes raked her from head to toe. "Not when you look like you do." Ariel felt her cheeks flare anew and she believed those words, fool girl that she was. It was difficult not to feel emboldened by the intensity of this man's gaze, the hint of a needy rasp in his deep voice. Throwing all common sense to the wind, Ariel raised her arms and opened them to Charles. The man seemed only too happy to oblige as he quickly finished shrugging from his coat and unwinding his cravat. Dropping both to the floor, he pounced upon her, carefully balancing his weight to press just enough of it against her aching nipples as his mouth covered hers once more. The hard length of one powerful thigh nudged her legs apart to rub ever so subtly against the growing moisture collecting at the juncture there. Her pelvis arched and searched for more pressure, but Charles would only allow her a taste before he retreated just far enough that she could not quite obtain that which her body desired. He flashed her a most wicked grin when she emitted a small, involuntary whimper of frustration; his mouth covered hers once more the next moment, his skillful tongue slipping between her lips once more to trace the fine edge of her teeth and tangle with hers. Ariel kissed him back, gaining confidence with every stroke of his tongue and softening of her muscles. Her legs fell open wider and he rewarded her with more pressure of his firm thigh against that secret place between them.

He laid himself a little more flush atop her and she experienced the thick, marble-like ridge of his manhood pressing through the layers of the fabric between them to brand the soft mound of her lower belly.

Before she had time to grow too nervous, Charles lifted his head just enough to speak against her mouth. "You may touch me." Kiss. "In fact..." Kiss. "I insist you do so." Another kiss that melted her limbs to the point she was afraid she would be unable to feel him if she did wrap her body around him.

To her ecstatic delight, she did feel the swell of his broad shoulders with her palms, she was able to trace the sharp lines of his collarbone beneath the fine linen of his crisp white shirt, and she could savor the slight undulation of the impressive muscles spanning his back with every one of his minuscule thrusts. She was rewarded with a sharp hiss of pleasure when she ran experimental nails down his spine and then up his trim sides and the bumps of his ribs. The response emboldened her in a new way.

"You seem to be rather sensitive as well."

The feral glint in Charles' eyes made her heart skip frantically in her breast.

"I think it's time we divest you of these cumbersome clothes." His tone was dangerous, but far from frightening. She floated upon this curious cloud of nerves and excitement, barely aware as Charles lifted her up once more and, in between more kisses, caresses, and nibbles, began to undress her with startlingly—or not-so-startlingly—practiced ease until she remained only in her thin shift, stockings, and garters. Charles pulled back and rose, bracing himself with one knee on the bed and the other foot on the floor as his eyes traced every one of her curves with animalistic appreciation. They lingered upon the swell of her hips and the dusky shadows of her nipples. Ariel sat up on her elbows and her rose-gold curls tumbled around her face and shoulders—the man really must have been a magician to remove her hairpins without her realizing! She nibbled her lip and made the sudden decision to ride out this wave of confidence.

"Will you remove your clothing as well, sir?"

One of his dark brows cocked at her question; the tilt of his lips made her weak all over again. Without speaking or removing his eyes from hers, Charles undid his cuffs and the closures along the front of his shirt, collecting the glinting silver fastenings in his large palm before setting them on the small table beside her bed. She swallowed hard when he untucked the garment from his breeches and slid it from his shoulders to reveal a chest the likes of which she hadn't thought existed in nature. He was all lean lines and angles hewn as if by Michelangelo's chisel. He was smooth save for a light dusting of dark whorls at the center of his chest. The defined ridges of his abdomen teased her ever so naughtily before they disappeared beneath the fitted waist of his breeches. Surely, her eyes must have been as wide as saucers, but Charles was kind enough—or savvy enough—not to comment or mock her inexperience.

"The next move is yours, Ariel." She hadn't thought the mixture of vowels and consonants comprising her name lent themselves to a purr, but Charles managed it with impressive ease.

Pulling her lips between her teeth, she slid to the edge of the bed and stood, her body so close to Charles' that she could feel the heat rolling off his naked flesh. She swiftly undid her garters and slid her stockings from her legs. Without pausing to overthink it, she lifted her shift over her head and added it to the growing pile of garments scattered near the bed—the tangible proof of her recklessly abandoned inhibitions.

Though she didn't look up into his face, she watched him take a few steps back and she could feel the caress of his gaze from head to toe. The room was warm, but she shivered. As a reflex, she crossed her arms over her ample bosom. The gesture was useless but somehow necessary. The heat of her flush seeped from her face to her throat, it warmed her chest and tinted the pale flesh of her breasts pink.

"It is natural for a woman to be shy the first time she is unclothed before a man," Charles murmured kindly. His tone was as warm as his molten eyes when she finally met them. "But you should never be ashamed."

"I am not ashamed," Ariel spoke as adamantly as possible, though she feared the slight warble gave her away. She knew she was not like other women—she was too tall, too curvaceous, too unconventional, too...her. She had come to love her body, but she also recognized that not everyone felt the same. She could have possessed the proportions deemed perfect in Society and she doubted she'd feel any differently about the situation, laid quite literally bare as she was. This was vulnerability in its rawest form. She didn't think she could weather it if Charles demonstrated even a flicker of hesitancy.

"I'm glad of it," he rasped hoarsely. "Because it would be a tragedy above all others for this body to be hidden away."

Her heart's pace redoubled. Surely he only said such things because he was being paid for the evening. Surely he said such things to all the women he was with.

But all of her mental ramblings were silenced when Charles' gaze raked over her, as palpable as if he'd touched her with the fiery brand of his fingers.

And then he really was touching her. He gently removed her arms from her breasts, which suddenly felt heavier beneath his assessing eyes.

His pupils dilated, nearly swallowing the irises whole.

"Give a spin," he whispered harshly with a small twirl of a finger in a gesture more lighthearted than its owner appeared.

Willing herself not to cross her arms again, Ariel did as she was told. She earned a guttural groan of appreciation when Charles spied the waterfall of her rose-gold curls tumbling down her back, ending just before the voluptuous mounds of her bottom. She would have completed her spin had Charles not stalled her with the whisper of a finger on the swell of her hip. Just that small touch was enough to send ripples of anticipation from her body. She stood still as a statue.

Waiting.

The pounding of her heart filled the stretching silence until she thought she would burst.

"Lean forward," Charles finally instructed, his voice balancing the sharp line between pain and composure.

She did so, canting her hips back until she was at a seventy-degree angle. It wasn't enough because he murmured a few reassuring, complimentary words as he used a palm to urge her forward until her palms were flat upon the mattress, her rear jutting out behind her shamelessly.

His large palms cupped the rounded swells of her bottom. His strong hands kneaded her, massaging the flesh and muscles. He nudged her feet apart and spread her wide and growled his pleasure at the sight, as deep and penetrating as thunder. She experienced another rush of liquid heat between her legs at the sound, the dampness increasing with shameless abandon.

"What a sight…" Charles rasped, his voice barely above a whisper. "May I touch you here?" His fingers slid incrementally toward the crevasse between her legs, the deep cleft of her bottom. Ariel swallowed and nodded wordlessly. Immediately, his hands came together, spreading her wider for his perusal. Two of his fingers dipped lower and he moaned at what he discovered.

"Just as I thought; so wet already." His touch was torturously gentle against her slick, swollen flesh. He traced her nether lips, caressed the damp curls at the crux of her sex, and swirled around her entrance, making her arch her spine and press back into his touch.

Charles inhaled sharply and released it on one drawn out, "*Fuck…*" The word was shockingly crude—made even more so on his blunt American tongue, but she was far from offended. Her heart tripped with excitement. His hand stilled, cupping her tightly, his fingers curling to enter her ever so slightly. "If only you knew how delicious you look, Ariel; what this view does to me."

Her heart pounded at the raw words, his haggard voice. She could believe him when he sounded like that—she gasped as he began to stroke her once more—and especially when he touched her like that.

One of his large palms pressed gently between her shoulder blades until she rested her cheek on her forearms. His knees nudged her thighs open wider as his hand trailed back up her spine, tracing the concave arch created by his manipulation. "That's it," he purred. "Such a good girl." It should have felt demeaning, but it only made her inner thighs quiver in anticipation. She felt both powerful and at his mercy… And when his hand dipped lower between her legs, his longest fingers discovered the most magical thing of all.

The firm, slick pressure against that sensitive bundle of nerves both melted her and made her clench. She gasped until her breath died in her throat. *That* was new. And thrilling. And wonderful. Despite the wave of delicious sensations, her thighs flexed in an attempt to close and protect her most secret of places, but Charles didn't allow it. His chuckle danced across her spine and his large palm kneaded the soft globe of her buttocks, the long fingers sinking into her flesh. He tsked at her. "I know you like it. I can feel how wet you are." Ariel felt her flush spread rapidly from her face to her throat and chest at his words.

And then he began to move those knowledgeable fingers of his, swirling and plucking and caressing and stroking her in ways she hadn't considered and unleashing sensations she hadn't known possible. Her body began to undulate; her hips pressed back into Charles until she made contact with the hard bulge in the front of his breeches. An appreciative sound rumbled behind her. "Almost, pet. You're nearly ready."

"Ready? For—oh!" She cried out in shocked pleasure when his thick thumb pressed inside of her while his nimble fingers continued teasing the pearl at the crux of her sex. She screwed her eyes closed and every one of her senses focused on what Charles was doing to her and how he made her feel. Her skin tingled, her muscles clenched and trembled, her toes curled, and her nails gripped the sheets so tightly she feared they would be shredded. The pressure was building uncontrollably in her core with every slick glide of Charles' fingers on her and in her. Her body clenched around him with every dragging stroke. She panted and rocked against his onslaught.

"Please," she whimpered desperately.

"Please, what?" Charles leaned over her and purred. She could only toss her head from side to side, unable to put words to her needs. Charles, however, seemed to know exactly what she craved. "This?" he growled, applying just the right pressure and rhythm to make her arch her back and sob as the world shattered around her. She buried her face in the coverlet, letting it absorb her cresting pleasure. Her body was wracked by the blinding, consuming fire Charles had unleashed within her. It was glorious and terrifying and life-altering.

She floated down slowly from the rapture, the feeling gradually returning to her quaking limbs, when the sound of rustling cloth reached her ears. She barely registered it before Charles' warm hands returned to her bottom. The unfamiliar tickle of crisp masculine hair on strong, muscular thighs grazed her skin and she vaguely recognized he'd shucked the remainder of his clothing so he was finally as bare as she.

"Tell me you still want this, Ariel," Charles demanded, gripping her flesh with desperate fingers. "Or tell me to stop now because, by God, I can't guarantee I have much self-control left in me." She was still too fuzzy to register the oddity of those words. "Say it now." Something thick and hard prodded the wet folds of her sex.

She moaned and pressed her hips back, eliciting a guttural groan from deep within Charles' chest when the tip of him inadvertently slipped ever so slightly into the entrance of her tight sheath.

"Say it," he hissed painfully, Ariel gasping in response to the sound and the stretching sensation. "Say it," Charles repeated even more forcefully.

"Yes, yes, yes…" she breathed again and again, her voice growing louder as Charles began to slowly push into her body, joining them, claiming her, changing her. The dew he'd coaxed from her body helped the way, but she was still impossibly tight, and he, impossibly large. Her body stretched around him and Ariel silently repeated to herself that her body had been made for this, but the insistent sting was growing ever more uncomfortable.

Then, Charles stopped.

She nearly lifted her head to ask him why, when she felt his large palms and strong fingers drawing languid designs upon the skin of her back, between her shoulder blades, down the channel of her spine, cupping and caressing the round globes of her rear. He began to knead her muscles, the only part of him moving were his hands as they danced across her muscles, massaging and melting her tension away like wax beneath a candle's relentless flame. Only when she was a pliable puddle once more did Charles resume pressing forward into her. There was a small, sharp rip of pain and then, he was seated fully within her.

"Are you well?" Charles panted, his warm hands gripping her hips tightly, the fingers digging into her flesh in a not-unpleasant way. She nodded her head, her curls obscuring her vision like a veil. It was all the encouragement Charles needed to begin moving.

The retreat and thrust began as a slow, insistent rhythm of deep strokes which somehow managed to remain gentle and ever careful of her tender flesh.

Ariel closed her eyes and, with a deep sigh, she let go. She gave herself over to the physical sensations of Charles behind her, touching her, deep inside her, rubbing some heretofore unknown place that made her vibrate from the inside out. Her ears were deaf to all except the soft sounds of the collision of slick flesh and Charles' erotic gasps and groans and murmurs of praise. Some of the words from his lips were unbearably naughty, others, unexpectedly sweet. He called her a goddess, perfection personified; he also told her he loved how wet she was for him, how it drove him mad with need.

She fisted her hands in the rumpled coverlet when he leaned forward to reach around her thigh, dipping his fingers between her dripping folds and caressing that secret pearl. A breath hissed between her teeth as he touched her hypersensitive flesh to begin once again the trembling climb toward that pinnacle of perfection where the stars shattered behind her eyes in blinding flashes of white ecstasy and her body simultaneously clenched and melted. Each pass of his fingers lifted her higher and higher, tearing gasps and cries of joy she didn't bother to smother against her arm or the mattress.

"Yes," Charles growled. "Let me hear you, Ariel." His words loosed a bolt of joy from her stomach to her limbs and back and, with it, a tremulous sob of pleasure. Something seemed to snap inside of Charles. His hands moved to clasp her hips in a deliciously bruising grip as he pounded into her from behind. Flesh smacked on flesh, the pendulous weight of the sac beneath his member striking her clitoris with every powerful thrust. She braced her forearms and arched back into him, meeting him thrust for thrust as he drove deeply, mercilessly into her tight sheath. "That's it. I knew you could take all of me. I knew it the moment I saw you." He pounded into her from behind. His power and strength should have been painful, but it made her feel both weak and powerful and brought her only pleasure so incredulous it was blinding. Charles was unleashed and it was glorious. His body and his presence seemed to devour her; he set her nerves, her senses, her body on fire. "Let me feel you come," Charles commanded. "I want to feel you clench around my—"

Ariel never heard the end because she was tipped over that precipice. She was falling head over heels, tumbling harder, farther, faster than she ever thought possible as Charles continued his brutal, relentless pace. Her body trembled and quaked and then, suddenly, she was tragically empty. There was a gravelly roar behind her and splashes of something hot and forbidden on her lower back, dripping down the curve of her bottom.

She was panting and shivering as the last tremors of joy vibrated through her limbs when a warm hand cupped her cheek and turned her head, the throbbing heat of a male body enveloped her. Soft lips covered hers in a tender, lingering caress.

"You are magnificent, Ariel..." The words were a warm whisper upon her lips and she knew they would echo throughout the halls of her mind for many, many years to come.

Before she knew it, she was wrapped within Charles' long, strong arms, feeling impossibly feminine and infinitely cherished. She sighed contentedly, both her mind and her body still contentedly coasting along the rivulets of passion to which Charles had introduced her. They remained just so for several long, comfortable minutes merely listening to the other's breathing and gradually slowing heartbeats when Ariel's eyes shot open.

This man was not her husband. They were not in a relationship of any sort. This was a business transaction, and the last thing she wished was for him to feel obligated to coddle her.

"You needn't linger, you know." Ariel was surprised to discover that her throat was a tad tender from the repeated cries of ecstasy Charles had coaxed from her.

"I beg pardon?" She could feel him lift his head to look down at her.

"I mean, I am certain you have elsewhere you would desire to be. It was…quite lovely to meet you, but I wouldn't wish to keep you."

She felt his broad chest huff in a silent scoff. A handful of heartbeats passed before he asked, "You paid for the entire night, did you not?"

"Well…yes…"

"Then the entire night you shall have."

Ariel tried to ignore the butterflies in her abdomen at his words. She settled for snuggling back into Charles' embrace and savoring what little time they had left.

Chapter Three

Charles believed Ariel to be asleep when her voice, leaden with exhaustion, reached up to caress his ears. "If you're American, why are you here in England?" The question was light, but contemplative, as if she'd mulled it over for quite some time before sleep had lowered her inhibitions enough to pose the query—leave it to her to view a man whom she believed to be a male prostitute enough of a human to want to get to know him.

He thought a moment before he responded, weighing the choices and debating if it would be easier to simply feign sleep. He decided against pretending, though, because she'd been nothing if not entirely open and genuine and vulnerable with him. The least he could do was answer her question with as much truth as possible.

"I was raised in Boston," he began in a low voice, tracing his thumb along the downy-soft curve of her shoulder. "But my cousin passed and there was some business only I could handle, so here I am."

"Have you been here long?"

"Not especially."

"You have no relatives?"

The question evoked a sudden and rather unexpected burst of memories. His mother, a saint and a martyr, an angel with delicate features and soulful eyes, who had died giving birth to a girl when Charles was eleven; his father, a cold man who viewed displays of emotion and affection as signs of weakness, the reason all the warmth in his life had been smothered as soon as his mother had breathed her last. For decades, Charles had believed his father's death would release the leaden weight in his chest; however, as he'd learned three years earlier at the old man's funeral, it had left him numb. His emotions had been so deadened from the constant threat of beatings at the sign of tears, hissed threats when laughter came too easily, that he'd merely watched them lower the box into the ground, cast a handful of soil upon it, then turned on his heel and went back to his offices to finish the day.

He took a second too long to reply and she looked up at him, concern coloring her eyes. "My apologies, you needn't answer that if you do not wish to. I—I realize this is very personal but…so is all of this…" She glanced pointedly down at their naked bodies and then back up to his face. "And it feels so strange to me to know nothing—" Charles placed the pad of his thumb against her lower lip to stall her words. One corner of his mouth raised uncontrollably. He made an educated guess that a typical male prostitute would not reveal this much about himself, but Ariel had no point of reference against which to compare this experience. And, so, he answered.

"No. I've no one." And the response was tragically true. He had no surviving siblings. Acquaintances rather than true friends. Colleagues rather than companions. No woman had ever enticed him enough to contemplate spending his life with her. He had his work as his lover, friend, and family. And now, he had a skewed sense of the self he'd worked so hard to cultivate all because a distant cousin had died without any direct heirs.

Charles traced her plump lip with his thumb, the tip just slipping inside and setting his blood back on the path to boiling.

"And you stayed here all by yourself? That seems so lonely," she said wistfully, her eyes searching his face with a sincerity that shook him.

He wanted to ask her if that seemed as lonely as a woman who was so disregarded and overlooked by Society that she had to hire a man to give away her virginity, but he didn't. Those words would have been in his father's cold, cruel tone...an echo from Charles' damaged past...and Ariel didn't deserve that. The man was dead and buried; his words deserved to be, too.

"I manage," he replied in a low tone. And he did. He'd learned to carve out an existence in the life laid out before him. Inheriting this dukedom had set him off-kilter, but he was determined to follow the path he'd charted and continue onward. He'd return to Boston and try to forget that he'd ever been to this dreary little island...but he somehow knew this woman lying against him would be much, much harder to forget.

"Oh, no! I couldn't possibly—"

"You most certainly *can*, and you most certainly *will*."

"I couldn't—"

"You can, *Ariel*."

Charles had been attempting to convince Ariel of the wisdom of his demand for the better part of ten minutes and his patience was wearing thin. Why couldn't she trust him about this? He was, after all, the supposed expert in this situation.

And this was something he'd craved with ravenous intensity since the moment he'd decided to continue with this farce.

Ariel sat up in bed and was clutching the thin coverlet to her breasts in an ineffectual shield. The pink flush bleeding from her cheeks to her throat stood out in stark contrast to the fine fabric. Her eyes were downcast in a mixture of contemplation and mortification at his proposition; he found he missed her eyes, though the gilded fan of her long lashes against her cheeks was rather entrancing. Propping himself up on an elbow, Charles stretched out an arm and gently turned her chin to face him.

"I assure you;" he began in a soft yet firm tone; "I have wanted nothing more—especially not since I saw your delectable bare flesh. And, if I may be so blunt, I want to see all of you and taste every bit of your dripping cunny." His cock twitched powerfully at her sharp inhalation. She nibbled her lower lip in an unconsciously enticing motion. His voice was barely above a growl when next he spoke; "And you wanted a thorough education, did you not? Let me taste you, Ariel." Her eyes slid down to his mouth and, finally, she nodded her head.

There was less than a fraction of a second between her assenting gesture and when he swiftly positioned himself flat on the bed. He then smoothly hauled Ariel from her nest of sheets so she straddled him with a knee on either side of his head. She yelped in surprise, but the sound quickly dissolved into nervous giggles.

"Grip the headboard," he instructed in a tone that brooked no questioning, his large palms cupping her rear, testing the soft pillows of flesh, spreading them and kneading them with reverence. She did so, and it canted her hips, opening her up wide to his gaze. His mouth watered as he memorized the dewy folds of her sex. He filled his lungs with the heady scent of her—the undercurrent of her lightly scented soap from an earlier bath lingering beneath the salt of their earlier coupling. "Now, come to me." She looked down at him with comically wide eyes but did not move. "Lower yourself," he demanded, his fingers digging into the lush flesh of her bottom to urge her down.

"I—I don't wish to suffocate you…" Her words were pained with embarrassment, but Charles's eyes flashed up to meet hers.

"Darling, if that is the way God wishes me to die, then I shall gladly do so. I shall perish a legend and be proud of it. In fact, it is a method of death I find far preferable to all others available." A small whimper of unwilling excitement eeked from Ariel's throat. "Now. Lower yourself onto me and let me taste you. I have been a very patient man and I believe I deserve a reward."

Charles sent up a silent prayer of thanks when Ariel finally lowered herself. She was tentative at first until he urged her flush with his face. Any apprehension she retained melted away when he began to use his lips and tongue to introduce her to a new kind of wicked pleasure. It wasn't long before she began to press herself against him, rocking her pelvis to seek out the teasing touches he offered. He took his time learning every inch of her, exploring every petal and fold, spearing his tongue deep within her slick channel to make her shudder and moan as she clamped her thick thighs around his head. Heat flooded his groin, bringing his burgeoning arousal to painful hardness with a speed unlike anything he'd ever experienced. He couldn't resist wrapping a fist around his throbbing member, gipping it nearly as tight as Ariel's body had earlier. He pumped his fist in time with the rocking of Ariel's hips against his mouth. Her entire body trembled and clenched, she cried out and threw her head back when he sucked on the swollen, sensitive nub at the crux of her sex. He moaned against her, the sound rumbling through his body to tickle her further.

He licked and nibbled, he sucked and swirled, he relished the sweet nectar dripping down his chin and collecting on his tongue like ambrosia from the gods. His hand pumped his erection harder, palming the head before squeezing the length from tip to root and back, again, and again, and again. Likewise, Ariel's movements became more desperate and her breathing more ragged. She was close…so close he could quite literally taste it. A few more practiced flicks of his tongue and she shattered. Charles closed his eyes and absorbed her climax with every one of his senses until he could take it no more.

She hadn't quite floated back down to earth when Charles, carrying Ariel with him, sat up and laid her on her back before entering her in one deep, rough thrust that stole the air from both their lungs. He swore he could see stars flying through the darkness behind his clenched eyes. Ariel's fingers grabbed at his arms and waist. It took him a moment to realize she was trying to pull him closer rather than push him away.

Well, he couldn't say no to that, could he?

Charles retreated from her tight sheath nearly to the tip before slamming back. He was held rapt by her dreamy expression, her plump lips parted in silent gasps as he began to pound into her. His eyes roved her flushed skin, the perfection of her bountiful bouncing breasts and their ripe berry nipples, the smooth curves and valleys of her luscious hips and abdomen.

Gripping her shapely ankles, he spread her legs wide to make her vulnerable to his powerful thrusts and give him an uninhibited view of the point where their bodies joined and glided. Charles was held rapt by the sight of his painfully turgid cock sliding in and out of her body, lulled into an erotic trance by the delighted gasps of this incredibly bold, sensual woman.

He leaned forward and groaned at the delicious new angle; his pelvis ground against her clitoris in just the right rhythm he'd already learned would set her aflame. He palmed her breasts and plucked at the hard buds of her nipples, earning him a cry of pleasure. And, when she came again, he followed not far behind. He ripped himself from her fluttering sheath and spilled his hot seed across her succulent breasts.

Chest heaving, Charles gazed down at the glorious sight of Ariel laid out beneath him like a nymph on the altar of a pagan god, her rosy-blond hair fanned out behind her head like a halo and her soft, curvaceous body a masterpiece of Renaissance art in the flickering light. His heart thudded against his ribs and his pulse rattled his bones. When her mouth tilted in a small smile of wonderment, it stuttered sharply.

Beautiful.

This woman was beautiful in every sense of the word; she was also driven, brave, sensuous, desirable, and she had no idea how dangerous she was.

It took Charles nearly thirty painful minutes of creeping around in the dark until he was able to successfully slip from the back door of the Townhouse to the mews, his cloak and hat in tow. He donned the garments to help him blend into the shadows as he slipped away, forcing himself to avoid glancing back at the rear of the brick building like a pitiful pining pup.

It had taken an otherworldly amount of strength and will to untangle Ariel's soft body from his and drag himself from her warm bed, but he knew he had to make his way through Mayfair to his own home before the sun rose. Already the sky was threatening to lighten to lilac and, soon, reality would overtake the feverish dream that was the previous night. Slipping through the streets, Charles believed with every fiber of his being that he would never see Ariel again…though a part of him was unaccountably deflated over this fact.

Chapter Four

Two days had passed since the night she'd spent with Charles and Ariel still couldn't believe no one could read the changes on her face.

She'd woken the following morning deliciously sore in new places; rubbing her thighs together produced an interesting ache where the short stubble on Charles's jaw had rubbed her intimately when he'd… Her cheeks flushed at the wicked memory and she'd pressed her legs together more tightly.

The actual day of her birthday came with rather less fanfare than the night before—it wasn't precisely the thing to be celebrated and called attention to when a woman turned thirty without any marital prospects to speak of. She did not see her brother until it was nearly late afternoon. Both pretended he hadn't been spotted returning from his mistress's home (disheveled and weary) just as she settled into her favorite chair in the library for a reading spell. Arnold, the Earl of Darby, greeted her with a kiss atop her head and dropped a small parcel in her lap.

"Happy birthday, dear sister," her brother smiled warmly and threw his large frame across the cushions of the sofa. They shared a similar build and stature, but the *ton* didn't seem to take issue with his appearance. Perhaps he was spared because he was a man or because he possessed a title; either way, she'd never felt it was quite fair.

"What is this?" Ariel grinned and set aside the book she'd been reading.

"You'll just have to open it, won't you?"

"You appear obnoxiously pleased with yourself, so it must be something wonderful."

Her brother simply replied with a lift of his shoulder and focused on fiddling with the gold signet ring he wore on his smallest finger.

Ariel recognized the paper and cobalt blue ribbon as belonging to one of the premier booksellers in London; the Ladies' Reading Society to which she belonged often ordered their materials from them.

Arnold was not an overly demonstrative sibling, so receiving a gift from him once each year was an occasion. Even so, he'd often defer to her "expertise" and simply gift her with additional funds to purchase a special gown or select a piece of jewelry for herself. The fact that he'd gone and purchased something for her was novel and touching.

She'd dropped several none-too-subtle hints about a particular collection of essays she'd been eyeing and, while it certainly was no garment or gem, Ariel didn't care. The fact that he'd—

Her fingers stilled when she revealed enough of the leather cover to read the embossed title.

"'A Good and Virtuous Lady's Guide to Comportment and Marriageability'?" The title alone nearly caused bile to rise in the back of her throat.

"Hemsley recommended it highly. Gave a copy to his sister and she had three offers in a fortnight."

"Because Amarintha is only eighteen years of age, biddable, and—while sweet—has fewer unique thoughts in her head than the poor pocket-sized dog she drags around." Ariel's annoyance rose as reality settled in her gut.

"No need to be unkind or ungrateful, Ari." Her brother frowned as if she'd stomped all over his gift and then spat upon it for good measure—as if he'd truly believed the book had been a kind and thoughtful gesture.

Ariel took a bracing breath and counted to five before she spoke again. "I appreciate the thought, Arni...but aren't I well past the stage of trying to reform enough so I might make a match?"

"I suppose three decades is rather long in the tooth..." he began thoughtfully; "however, I choose to remain optimistic. As should you, dear sister." He sounded almost chastising as if *she* were the one who had just likened herself to a nag fit for nothing but being turned out to pasture.

"This is optimism, then?" She did her best to omit the disdain from her voice as she held up the book, but she doubted she was entirely successful.

"I should think so."

"And you believe this book will contain anything I have not already been trained, coached, or shamed to do in these past three decades?"

Arnold finally sat up to face her squarely, rather than reclining like a recalcitrant wastrel. "How do you expect me to know? It was a book and you like books. It came recommended, so I purchased it. I see now that I was foolish to believe I might present you with a gift which might also serve to assist you in your predicament."

Ariel's fingers tightened on the leather-bound book and every fiber of her being wished she could toss it into the hearth and watch it burn. Leave it to Arni to reduce her existence to merely "liking books." It wasn't the first time he'd been dismissive of her enjoyment of the written word. The book she held was about as far removed from Greek mythology and new essays on women's rights as blancmange was from one of Cook's raspberry-lemon tarts smothered in clotted cream and sugar crystals. Her brother had spent years attempting to water down what he believed were the reasons she was unmarriage-able.

At sixteen, she'd gently corrected one of Arnold's friend's references to the story of Narcissus and Echo in a poem he had penned and then presented to them. Her brother had then pulled her aside and told her she couldn't possibly believe anyone would take her seriously, so there was no point in speaking up.

At twenty, she'd merely meant to participate in a dinner conversation being had regarding a current court matter of a woman wishing to retain property after the death of her husband. When she'd finished citing several poignant and highly-relevant cases and essays, the entire table was silent. The look in Arnold's eyes told her everything she knew she would hear later: Men did not enjoy being made to appear uneducated on a topic, nor was it becoming for a woman to appear so knowledgeable.

She could dance as well as any lady of breeding—in fact, she quite enjoyed it—but it didn't help a man's ego when his partner was a head taller than he…not that there was anything Ariel could have done about *that*, but she was still somehow at fault.

These were only a few of what she knew her brother (and Society) viewed as her myriad of sins.

Ariel didn't doubt that the book in her hand wholeheartedly corroborated Arnold's stance and she would be, yet again, condemned for having a brain in her head and meat on her bones. How many times had she heard that a woman must be meek, soft-spoken, and defer to a man's knowledge and guiding hand; she must place her husband and her home before all else, she must take great pains to follow Society's standard of beauty to the letter? Merely thinking about it made Ariel's stomach churn like a boiling sea.

"So nice to hear that you view my life as a predicament," she muttered; a much more muted response than the one she'd wanted to deliver, but she'd long learned when to save her breath. To her surprise, this response elicited some tenderness from Arnold. Her brother rose and crouched down beside her.

"Don't be so downtrodden, Ari, you know I cannot stomach it." He took her hands in his and set aside the blasted book. "You're no burden, you know that? I only want you to have the life you deserve." His fingers squeezed hers and he placed a quick brotherly peck on her forehead. "I'll return the book if it bothers you and I'll buy you twenty in its place if it'll make you smile. It was not my intention to make you feel this way today, of all days."

She gave him a tight smile. Arnold could be obtuse, selfish, and too prone to caring about Society's opinions, but he wasn't a bad brother. At only eighteen months apart in age, they were closer than most siblings. She knew he loved her, but that didn't change the fact that his comments and jabs left invisible bruises and sore spots. This book just happened to whack a particularly tender one.

"I have no need of twenty more books," she said, attempting levity.

"Really?" His brows rose in mock shock and then he glanced around the room. "I think there might still be some room up near the ceiling…way over in that corner."

Ariel couldn't resist giggling. She'd amassed quite the collection of books and had gradually filled every shelf in the room. The house may belong to the title and her brother, but these books…these were her treasures.

"Maybe one or two, then," she conceded and was rewarded with a warm smile and a pat on the hand.

The rest of Ariel's birthday went more smoothly. Two of her friends, Alaina, the Duchess of Morton, and Meredith, Viscountess Sommerfeld, surprised her after luncheon and whisked her away for a few hours of shopping on Oxford Street. Together, they traversed the popular area, arm-in-arm, ducking into whichever storefront caught their fancy. In addition to two books intended to replace the atrocity Arni had given her, Ariel wound up with a new pair of fine gloves and allowed the Lady Morton to talk her into purchasing a golden broach in the shape of an owl with emerald eyes so green they appeared to glow —the symbol of Athena, Ariel's favorite of the Greek goddesses. She represented wisdom, a wealth of bravery, resourcefulness, and, as a virgin goddess, she had no children of her own so she often formed other bonds in place of a spouse or offspring. Ariel liked to think she had lived her life similarly. Her entire remaining family consisted of her brother, and he would someday need to marry and start a family of his own to carry on the title; she would be relegated to the role of spinster aunt on the periphery. She'd been adopted into a clutch of women and, likewise, she'd adopted them in return. She'd made her own family. And, up until the prior night, she'd also been a virgin.

Her cheeks flared once more as the memories washed over her in a pleasant, erotic tide.

She'd woken that morning feeling forever changed after her night with Charles. Though she liked to believe herself mostly levelheaded, there were several long moments in the watery morning light when she'd wondered to herself how she was supposed to go back to her old life after experiencing such rapture at his hands. How was she supposed to move forward? How was she supposed to forget about him and resume her respectable spinster lifestyle? How could she be content knowing pleasure of that magnitude existed in the world...and she would likely never taste it again? Her eyes had been forever opened to it and there was no turning back.

She realized it made her the worst sort of pathetic ninny, but, even now, she couldn't help but feel that she had shared a connection with Charles, that he'd understood her and liked her as well.

Ariel shook her head to knock some sense into herself. Of course, Charles hadn't felt that way—if that was even his real name! It had been one night and that was it.

One night to last her forever.

The ballroom was abuzz with excitement, the low hum of voices rising and falling like the drone of an excited bee flitting from bloom to bloom. London's elite had gathered for a birthday ball and Arnold had insisted Ariel accompany him; he'd missed a meeting with the guest of honor and wanted to apologize in person—though, upon their arrival, he'd promptly relinquished her into the care of her friend, Caroline, Marchioness Brinley, and ducked off to the room set aside for cards and drinks. She and Caro were taking a turn around the room, waiting for the duke's arrival, when Ariel was suddenly tugged into a secluded corner.

"I simply must know," Caro gripped her hands, her wide hazel eyes sparkling. "How did the other night go?"

"Caro..." Ariel groaned and glanced around to confirm they were well out of earshot of other guests. Her cheeks began to burn furiously and she barely resisted the urge to fan her face. The last thing she wished to do was draw attention to them.

"Well you aren't offering up any details and I've been desperate!" she hissed, not unkindly. "I helped facilitate this little rendezvous and I feel entitled to at least know if it was everything you were hoping for." Ariel chewed her lower lip thoughtfully. Caro was right; Ariel wouldn't have been able to procure Charles' company without Caro's connections. Her husband's illegitimate half-brother had married a very sweet young lady…whose mother happened to run the most illustrious and scandalous bordello in London. It was all a very complex, thrillingly scandalous story better saved for another time.

Ariel flushed even more deeply and finally admitted that the evening was so much more than even her wildest imaginings. Caro practically squealed in delight for her friend.

The things Ariel had done…the things Charles had done to her… made her skin flush and just thinking about it made the flesh between her legs grow damp. She'd been brave enough to revisit the memories and try her hand at pleasuring herself. While the memories of Charles' touch did bring her to climax, it was not quite the same as having his hands and his mouth on her. She nearly shivered from the memories.

"So, Adonis lived up to his reputation, then?" Caro asked, wagging her perfectly arched brows a little. Though she was a respectable lady and a mother now, it wasn't difficult to see what a hellion she'd been even a few years prior. She'd been persona non grata amongst respectable circles, but her marriage to another former hell-raiser and subsequent motherhood had gone a long way toward making her more respectable in the eyes of most of Society. Her closest friends, however, knew a bit of the old Caro remained.

"I suppose Charles was an Adonis," Ariel replied thoughtfully, his handsome features playing before her mind's eye.

"Charles? Emily said he went by Adonis." Caro gave a little frown. "Oh? Perhaps Charles is his real name?"

Caro shook her head. "I'm told they never use their true names. Blond? Tall? Blue eyes? Emily inquired about your tastes, but I wasn't sure. He sounded more than passably handsome from her description." Ariel's stomach grew uneasy; Caro continued. "Perhaps he looked different in the dark and just decided to offer you a mundane name to make you more comfortable?" Caro offered. Just as Ariel's confused mind began to pick up speed, Caro grabbed her upper arm. "Oh, look! The duke is arrived!"

Ariel's mind was whirring so quickly she barely had time to register the steadily rising excitement surrounding them. It made some sense that Charles—Adonis...whatever his name was—may have used a different name with her. But then why would Caro have believed his appearance was supposed to be so very different? He was certainly tall, but there was nothing blond about his hair, nor had his eyes been blue. She'd stared into them enough to memorize the honey-gold rings around his pupils.

Ariel missed her friend's next words, but she did her best to respond with a weak smile and look in the direction to which Caro was gesturing. Their fellow guests were gathered like a swarm around a man whom Ariel couldn't quite see for all the plumage and flower arrangements. The duke gradually made his way through the crowd, greeting guests and accepting well wishes, and Ariel caught glimpses of broad shoulders and dark, curly hair...

"I met him at Lady Morton's dinner last month when you had that head cold," said Caro. "If I weren't a very happily married mother, I certainly would have tipped my cap at that tall, dark American."

"A—American?" Ariel had known the new duke to be an American—all of London did—but this, coupled with the odd conversation about Adonis made Ariel's knees weak. Her stomach lurched uncontrollably.

It couldn't possibly be.

There was simply no way.

Improbable.

Unthinkable.

She hardly heard Caro speaking over the growing deafening roar in her ears. She watched the dark head grow nearer, along with her unease. She didn't want to look, but she knew she had to. She had to prove to herself just how foolish she was being. Surely there was no way fancy man Charles was—good lord, he was the Duke of Ryton!

Chapter Five

The party was by far the most extravagant birthday celebration Charles had ever had. The day had lost all its meaning when his mother died and it had become just another day on the calendar. His cousin's widow, however, was determined not to allow his thirty-third birthday to slip by unnoticed. Indeed, it seemed as if she'd gone well above and beyond to give him an experience worthy of all the years he'd spent avoiding celebrations. In fact, Eugenia seemed to revel in it.

She had been prepared to move from the expansive home upon Charles' arrival from America, but he'd immediately made it clear that he wanted nothing of her life to change. She would continue living as she had as the duchess and he would ensure she was provided for. Grateful beyond words, she remained in residence and made it her mission to treat Charles as her adopted son, taking him around London and introducing him to her friends and other notable connections.

Charles had gradually developed the suspicion that Eugenia harbored a secret hope that Charles would make London his home…but that road would only lead to disappointment.

He did not doubt she knew Charles would have put a stop to the extravagance of this celebration if he'd caught wind of it, which was precisely why she'd organized it in secret. Eugenia had been so pleased to pull it off that Charles hadn't had the heart to send everyone out of his house. Faced with an expectant crowd of people he barely knew, he took a deep breath and prepared himself for an interminable evening filled with fuss and stuffy conversation.

The dowager had done her best to welcome him with warmth and kindness, it was the least he could do in return; especially because he would be leaving in less than two weeks.

He cut a swath through the crowd, nodding and exchanging pleasantries. If he was weary of this farce in London, he almost dreaded how he'd be received back home where dukes were as mystical and uncommon as unicorns. Even if he refused to use his title, he didn't doubt the word had already spread. His life would be irrevocably altered no matter what continent he was on. He'd made it halfway across the room when the shattering glass drew his gaze. Instead of a shamefaced servant, however, the woman he saw made the world go silent…

And, when her wide eyes met his, the room's din came crashing down around him all at once.

Ariel.

"Shit," he muttered, his heart suddenly pounding against his ribcage like a battering ram. He opened his mouth to say her name, but she brushed off her companion and whirled away before he could. She moved with impressive speed and had ducked from the room before he could make it two strides. Not caring how rude it was, Charles shoved through countless guests trying to both verbally and physically grab his attention. He knew he had to reach her before she left or he'd never have another chance. He couldn't call upon her at her brother's house—at least, not without setting tongues wagging—and she would likely turn him away anyway. There were a thousand ways for her to avoid him and very few options left to him if he wished to try to make things right.

Driven by his need to reach her, Charles trod on toes and took advantage of his title; these Brits would forgive a great deal when one's name was as lofty as his. But Ariel was nowhere in sight by the time he reached the hallway. It took several moments for his eyes to adjust to the dimmer lighting, but he thought he caught a glimpse of blue-green skirts turning the corner. He'd learned the general layout of the house by then and knew she could reach the front door, hail her carriage, and leave in a relatively short amount of time by cutting through the daffodil-yellow sitting room. Under no circumstances could he allow that to happen. Having her slip through his fingers was unthinkable.

He'd tried to deny it to himself over and over again, but he'd thought of little else other than her smile and her eyes and her body the last few days. When he saw her in the ballroom, he'd been unaccountably pleased, his heart and stomach doing a little flip-flop dance around one another.

He cursed the slick soles of his boots—designed more for form than function—as he nearly collided with a table and crystal vase during a particularly sharp turn.

"Ariel," he hissed as loudly as he dared, not wanting to yell lest he alert the staff or other guests. The last thing either of them needed was an audience. Charles cursed again. "Ariel," he called slightly louder that time.

Ariel's strides were long, but his were longer. He was rewarded by a solid view of teal floral skirts just as they disappeared into a room. Had she turned right, she'd have reached the proper sitting room and her quick escape; this turn, however, led her away from the front of the house. He knew he had her.

Charles burst through the door into the darkened room. Only a sliver of silver moonlight seeped between the drapes, but it was all he needed to catch sight of Ariel's shimmering rose-gold hair, the ringlets spilling down her right shoulder like molten ore. She had her back to him as she attempted to wrench open another door on the other side of the room, but it didn't budge. A rapid round of rather creative curses poured from her pretty lips.

"I believe a key is more likely to open that door than curses," Charles said, a light pant to his voice only partially due to his mad dash after her. Being alone with her once more was doing strange things to his pulse.

Her shoulders rose nearly to her ears and stiffened, but she did not turn around. The silence between them was leaden. Charles was morbidly curious to see how long she would allow it to last.

"Ariel," he finally said; "at least hear me out."

She whirled on him then, all glorious rage and spitfire. "Don't you dare use my name as if we were so familiar," she practically growled.

"I would think we're quite familiar."

Her cheeks stained an even darker shade and he knew it was precisely the wrong thing to say.

"Familiar?" she snarled and stalked toward him a couple of steps. He tried not to focus on how delectable her bosom looked swathed in that low-cut bodice—now was not the time, nor the place, no matter that a part of him was childishly thrilled at seeing her once again when he'd never thought it would come to pass. "You are the basest of beings. The verist of swindlers. The—the—my *God*, you are the Duke of Ryton." She loosed a loud bark of incredulous laughter at the irony and flung her hand in his direction. Charles didn't think they'd been followed, but it wouldn't do to be discovered. He needed her to keep her voice down. He held up a palm in what he hoped was a calming gesture.

"Please, let me explain," he said in an even, low tone.

"Explain?" Ariel demanded much more loudly than he would have preferred. "How could you possibly explain this?" A door down the hall closed with a thud. It was likely a servant slipping down the back stairwell to retrieve something, but Charles couldn't chance it...he couldn't allow Ariel to chance it. "There isn't anything you could say —" There was simply no preventing it. Charles cut off her tirade with one hand on her arm and the other palm clapped over her lips. She glared at him with those striking eyes and clasped his forearm to free herself, but he was still much stronger than she.

"I need you to listen," he spoke close to her ear, trying to ignore her heady scent. "I can explain all of this, but we need to go somewhere quiet." He felt her mouth shift beneath his palm. "And if you bite me, I promise to bite back," Charles growled. Her lips stilled, but the fire still burned in her eyes.

He needed to take her somewhere they could speak uninterrupted without the risk of damaging her reputation—anywhere there might be a locked door and they wouldn't be quickly discovered. Her nails bit into his arm through his coat as he hauled her along with him out into the dim hallway. He didn't feel good about dragging her along with him as he dashed further toward the back of the house and into the room that had once been the study of the old duke. Charles had yet to spend any real time there other than to peruse some dusty papers, but he did know with complete certainty that there was a solid working lock on the door and it was far from the party in the ballroom. He toted Ariel along with him, the last few strides going more smoothly when it seemed she realized the futility of her physical resistance. He pressed the door closed and turned the mechanism to barricade the room. Ariel immediately spun away from him and stomped out of his reach.

"Of all the impertinent, ill-mannered—"

"Yes, I believe we've established that you don't much care for me at the moment. May we move on?" He crossed his arms over his chest, watching as Ariel emitted a sound dangerously close to a growl and stalked away from him. "Now, will you allow me to explain?" he repeated, his patience thinning like ice beneath the growing heat of his frustration.

"As if you could possibly provide me with any excuse that would lessen my anger," she scoffed. Charles' hands balled into fists.

"Of course, I cannot blame you for your anger, ma'am…but I can assure you there was no premeditation or nefarious plotting on my end."

"Unlikely." She whirled away and Charles could help himself no longer; he was tired of chasing her through the damned house. His long stride devoured the space between them, effectively backing Ariel against the mahogany wainscoting and caging her in with his palms pressed flat against the wall on either side of her.

"You are an intelligent woman, Ariel. How could I have known before arriving upon your doorstep that you had hired a man for the evening?" Though the lighting was poor, he could still see the deepening flush upon her cheeks. The little minx refused to be cowed, however, and he found he admired her greatly when she proudly tilted her chin up and met his eyes squarely.

"You will address me as *Lady* Ariel. I did not give you leave to use my given name."

Charles released an undignified sound from his nose. "I seem to recall otherwise."

"I permitted Charles. You are the Duke of Ryton; a different man entirely."

His jaw clenched. She'd struck a deeper nerve than she'd intended. This was the crux of the issue Charles took with his new title. He was viewed as a different man in every way. What would it take for someone to see that he was still just that—a man?

Their bodies were so close he could feel the heat rolling off her and it took everything he had not to press himself against her bountiful curves...the very body he'd dreamt about each night since leaving her bed.

He closed his eyes to regain control, but it did no good when his deep inhalation only filled his lungs with Ariel's scent. His abdomen clenched and his cock twitched in anticipation.

"I need you to hear me and listen." His voice was rough as sawn wood and, when he opened his eyes once more, he saw Ariel's eyes on his face. Unless he was mistaken, there was an unwitting tenderness there. Her mind was on a similar track to his, whether she wished it or not. "You were never supposed to discover my real identity," he began. "It was supposed to be one night and we were never going to encounter one another again."

*****

Ariel was instantly mortified by this man's words, but fury quickly overtook it. "So you stumbled upon an opportunity and thought to lie your way into my bed before running off for a laugh when you were finished?" Angry tears burned behind her eyes.

"That wasn't it at all."

"Then what was it? Pity? I want none of it—oh how you must have laughed at me!"

"Ariel," the duke growled, even though she'd told him to stop using her name. She loathed it, but it still sent her stomach fluttering. "The fact that you feel that way drives me mad. I lied about nothing that night other than the reason I'd arrived on your doorstep. I truly was there only to discuss the purchase of a horse from your brother, but I allowed you to take the lead when I realized the error that had been made." Ariel's cheeks flushed so deeply they burned. "I believed I was doing you a favor."

"Well, thank you for your kind and generous soul, Your Grace." Her every word dripped with facetiousness.

"Listen to me!" he barked and her lips snapped shut. When all was said and done, she truly knew very, very little about this man effectively holding her hostage in the study in his home. He was tall and she knew firsthand his strength; he'd been able to lift her with surprisingly little effort. And now she also knew he was a duke with more power in his little finger than she could ever dream of wielding. "I made an instantaneous decision to be the safer, better choice for you in your circumstances than a random male prostitute or courtesan— whatever term you Brits use. I wanted to protect you." The adamancy in his voice at the last was striking. "I admit what I did was out of a twisted sense of chivalry and, yes, desire… None of it was a chore in the least." Ariel's stomach began flipping all over again. "I lied about nothing when we were in your bedroom. Nothing." The dark pools of his eyes focused on her mouth, where she was currently nibbling on her lower lip. This seemed to set him over some dangerous edge and his restraint snapped. "Here is your evidence if you don't believe me," he growled, wrenching her hand down to cup the thick, hard ridge of his erection straining against the fabric of his breeches. The solid heat of his aroused flesh against her palm was enough to bring all the memories back to the forefront of her mind—whether she wanted them or not—and her knees became weak. She continued to meet Charles' eyes unflinchingly and kept her hand there against him even after he released her.

"Why?" The question slipped out on a breath, barely above a whisper.

"Because I couldn't resist. Because I wanted to." A muscle in his jaw flexed. "Because I couldn't walk away knowing your first time with a man—your first kiss—was going to be thrown away on a man who had had a hundred women and couldn't cherish them as the gifts they truly were. You deserved so much more than that…even if you never knew the truth of it." Charles cleared his throat before continuing. "The last thing I wanted to do was cause you shame or pain over it. I admit it was selfish—I was even aware of that at the time—but I wanted those gifts for myself…and how can you blame me when you are as captivating and desirable as you are?"

Ariel's mind went blank. All rational thoughts halted and her heart took over.

She believed him.

She shouldn't have done so—by all accounts, she should have slapped him, kicked him in the shin, and fled from the room—but there was something in his eyes, something about feeling the evidence of his desire for her once more, the pained honesty in his words that urged her to stand on her toes and press a gentle kiss to his lips.

Charles seemed only too happy to accept the gesture, as it immediately morphed into something more passionate. His tongue plunged into her mouth, rasping against hers in an insistent, seductive rhythm. He instantly pressed the hard length of his body against her, crushing her comfortably against the wall. Trapping her.

Her arms wound around his neck of their own volition, tugging him down to meet her greedy lips. She sighed in pleasure. Oh, how she'd missed the taste of him. And to have him kissing her with his body against hers once again was a sinful delight she'd never thought to experience. His pelvis rocked against her, reminding Ariel of just what awaited. A whimper of need escaped her throat, snapping what little restraint remained in Charles.

The cool air caressed her stockinged legs as the hem of her skirts was rucked up higher and higher. Deft fingers discovered the slit in her drawers. Her knees nearly gave out completely in response to the satisfied groan Charles emitted upon discovering how wet she was already. She might have been embarrassed had he not been so blatantly pleased.

He thrust his two longest fingers deep inside her, both of them gasping at the sensations unleashed.

"God, I've missed this," he moaned against the hammering pulse in his throat. Her eyes snapped open when she thought she heard him murmur, "I've missed *you*, Ariel," against the tops of her breasts, but she convinced herself she'd only heard what she wished to and focused on the stroking of his fingers and tongue. She cried out and arched forward when he curled his fingers, caressing somewhere inside that set her senses on fire. The pressure began to build and her whimpers filled the air. There was a slight pause as Charles freed himself from his breeches, hooked an arm beneath one of her legs, and thrust into her hard and deep.

"Charles!" she squealed, and he rewarded her with the relentless onslaught of his body on hers. Her fingers clutched his shoulders, holding onto him with all her strength. He was taking her hard, forcefully, but she welcomed the pounding, desperate lovemaking. She needed it, body and soul. She wanted to be claimed by him, marked as forever his. She loved it.

"Yes, Charles, *yes!*" Her guarded heart began to splinter. She pulled his head down to hers, pressing her forehead against him and meeting his passion-glazed eyes. Their panting breaths mingled in the small space between their lips.

"You amaze me," Charles breathed. "So sweet. So good." He stretched her and filled her, but it wasn't enough. She wanted to take every bit of him into her body, to absorb him and take him with her for all eternity.

"Please," she sobbed; "More...please, Charles."

The corners of his lips turned up in the most wicked grin Ariel had ever seen. "Anything for you." His mouth slanted over hers and his large hands clutched her hips, holding her immobile as he increased both the pace and depth of his thrusts, filling her again and again and again, relentlessly and mercilessly pushing her higher and higher

His mouth broke free from hers to press his lips to her ear. He told her how beautiful she was, how well she pleased him, how he desired to please her. Charles maintained his steady rhythm until, finally, Ariel shattered. She became a mass of trembling muscles and tingling limbs as wave after wave of pleasure crashed over her, threatening to drown her in bliss. Charles' words from the other night floated through her mind; she would gladly die in that moment, in the steady arms of this man.

Charles' rhythm stuttered and broke; he tore himself from her body, spilling his seed on the virgin expanse of her thighs with a guttural groan.

Ariel's eyes were closed, her body still wracked with the aftershocks of her climax when the soft press of Charles' lips caressed her damp forehead.

And Ariel knew she was ruined for all other lovers, had she been wont to take one in the future. No other man would make her feel as Charles did. With him, she felt desired and strong.

For his part, Charles experienced the sobering realization that he would never want another woman as he did Ariel. This wild, uninhibited, intelligent woman drove him mad with need.

When he regained feeling in his legs once more, Charles set them to rights and guided Ariel to the nearby sofa. She collapsed into a heap of skirts and satisfaction, smelling intoxicatingly of jasmine and sex. He chuckled before sitting beside her and nestling her curves against his side. He was both unnerved and comforted by the fact that she fit so well there beneath his arm, her head leaning against the side of his chest, her hand resting casually on his abdomen. He was not a small man and so many women he'd met over the years appeared breakable or too fragile in both body and spirit. That was most certainly not Ariel…

"Does this mean you forgive me?" he asked with more quiet confidence than he felt. There had been such genuine pain and anger in her eyes—rightly earned, of course—and a part of him was concerned that she would never accept what he had done. He hadn't been lying before; it had been wrong and selfish…but he regretted nothing. And he never would.

His heart froze and then redoubled when she looked up at him. The apples of her cheeks were tinged pink, her full lips were puffy from his kisses. And she was beautiful.

"I don't know if I've reached forgiveness, but I certainly have more understanding of what you did," she admitted softly. He couldn't resist running his thumb along the curve of her jaw and the soft roundness of her cheek.

"I never meant you any harm, Ariel."

She nibbled on her lower lip for a moment before responding. "I think I believe that."

"You believe, or you know?" he asked, raising a brow at her and loving the way her lips split into a grin. "One implies a level of certainty I would hope you'd have by now."

"We have only met two times, sir." His heart throbbed when she met his banter. "I don't believe I know you well enough for anything of certainty."

"And yet…" His eyes raked her body from head to toe and back before lowering his tone to a much more suggestive register. "I feel as if I know a few things about you with some certainty."

She flushed and swatted at him, earning another chuckle. My, but it felt good to let his guard down, especially with her. Had he ever jested so easily with a lover before? With anyone? Charles cleared his throat and decided he needed to move toward safer grounds.

"This is interesting," he said, touching the broach she wore pinned to the slightly crooked neckline of her gown. It began as an excuse to touch her, but the glint of the owl's emerald eyes caught his gaze.

"A birthday present," she replied gently.

"An admirer?" The question was posed in a light tone, but there was an undeniable pang of jealousy in his gut at the thought.

She responded with a small laugh through her nose. "If it had, then I wouldn't have had to…well…" She shrugged halfheartedly and glanced up at him from beneath her lashes.

If she'd had an admirer, then she needn't have hired a male prostitute for the evening…and they never would have met. "I purchased it for myself."

He cleared his throat, embarrassed at the unfortunateness of his query. "So, are you a budding ornithologist or do you simply have an unnatural affection for owls?"

"Neither," she replied, tracing the delicately wrought feathers on the golden wings. "The owl is one of the symbols of the Greek goddess Athena. I've loved Greek myths and legends ever since I was a little girl; she is my favorite."

"The goddess of wisdom. How appropriate." He thoroughly enjoyed the shy smile with which she rewarded him. "And what fascinates you about these ancient gods?"

"The grand stories, the way their existences and experiences tie in with life and nature. I find it comforting, the surety the ancient Greeks had in knowing the sun would rise with Helios and his chariot; that Spring would come with the return of Persephone, no matter how bleak the winter."

"And what of Athena? What drew you to her?" Charles hooked his finger in the neckline of her gown just behind the owl, his fingertip nestling in the warm crevice between her breasts. He gave a tiny tug while he filled his lungs with her scent and held it within his chest.

"She sprang from her father's head fully formed after Zeus suffered a horrible headache," she answered with a giggle. "My father always said I did the same to him with my incessant questions—he said it with love, of course. She gave humans the sciences and crafts. Athena was brave and wise and needed no man to make her whole." Her eyes darted to his eyes and then his mouth before looking away.

"All admirable traits," Charles mused. "But just because a woman does not need a man does not mean she cannot want him." Ariel's arresting eyes met his once more. "And it does not mean she cannot take what she wants and remain an independent woman."

"Rather radical notions."

He lifted a shoulder dismissively. "What can I say? America is more progressive without a monarchy." This earned him a musical laugh.

"Somehow I doubt even your upstart country is *that* progressive." They both laughed until Charles tugged her closer to press a sweet, lingering kiss upon her lips.

Her eyes fluttered open and he found the next words spilling from his lips before he could overthink them. "I leave for Boston in nine days and I would like to spend a great portion of my remaining time here with you, Ariel. Is that amenable?"

Her jaw dropped open in shock and it was all he could do not to lean forward and kiss her again. He settled for tucking an errant curl back into her coiffeur. "If it's that abhorrent an idea then you need only—"

"No! That is…no… It isn't abhorrent."

"Then, is that a yes?" Charles tried to deny to himself just how hopeful he was.

"And then you will board a ship bound for America?" He couldn't tell if she was contemplative or disappointed, so he simply nodded.

This was what he'd always planned. He had no desire to move to England. Of course, it couldn't be helped that he would have to make the occasional trans-Atlantic trip every so often, but—as he reminded himself each time he looked into Ariel's eyes—he had a life in Boston. He had never been a man who had dreamed of grandeur. He hadn't been elated when he'd been informed of his inheritance; he'd been terrified and angry. It was inconvenient and created a whole slew of new problematic situations for his life and his business.

Then again…

Without it, he never would have known this woman living an ocean away.

"You needn't answer right at this moment if you need to think it over, but I hope you will consider it."

"Yes."

Charles' heart clenched, but he maintained a stiff upper lip, just as his father would have expected. "Right, then send a note when you decide—" He froze when she placed a hand upon his arm.

"I mean, yes. I would very much like to spend time with you, Charles." It was the first time she'd said his name since learning of his true identity and Charles found he liked it very, very much, indeed.

Chapter Six

It was agreed that they would meet at the Ryton Townhouse at the next opportunity—they did not have that much time to waste, after all. Luckily for Ariel, her brother spent much of his time away from home, so it wouldn't be all that difficult for her to slip out unnoticed. Charles confirmed the dowager duchess planned to visit her sister for a few days, so they would have the sprawling ducal home to themselves. Well, minus the several dozen or so employees in the household. Charles had then escorted her back through the halls to the ball being thrown in his honor and, on the way, he explained that it wouldn't be that difficult for them to avoid servants. Ariel wasn't so sure, but she decided to trust him and agreed to the plan before she ducked back into the room. Charles followed several minutes later.

Caro had been concerned about Ariel's abrupt departure from the ballroom, but Ariel had assured her it had merely been a brief bout of queasiness that had quickly resolved. It was difficult for her to remain calm when Caro then insisted upon introducing Ariel to the American

Duke, as everyone had dubbed him. Gone was the man who'd made passionate love to her in the shadows of this study. This man was still dangerously handsome, but cooler and more refined. It was a thrilling secret between them; she read it in the burning coals of his eyes as he took her hand and kissed it, as he calmly accepted her belated birthday felicitations. It was everything she could do not to melt into a puddle right then and there.

She hadn't stopped thinking about that moment…or their interlude in the study just prior. And she had practically counted the hours until her brother left and she could slip away. It was thrilling, particularly having waited three decades for her very first clandestine meeting, her first lover. She was practically giddy as she left her home and followed a circuitous route several streets over back to Charles' home. It was early enough in the day that there weren't too many people about, other than servants running their errands and the occasional nanny with her charges. It was still unfashionably early for calling, but that was the point. She was fairly confident no one took much note of her; she had worn her simplest dress of mint green muslin devoid of lace and beadwork, plain cap sleeves and scooped neckline, with only a simple embroidered floral hem. It was far less extravagant than many women of her station wore out, but she didn't mind. She felt pretty, and she hoped Charles would think the same.

Following Charles' instructions, she went 'round back to meet him by the mews. The buildings were all immaculately kept and the cobblestones meticulously swept. The home she shared with her brother was nothing to sniff at, but this was practically a palace.

She stood near the garden gate with its high brick wall over which she could just see the tops of the sculpted shrubberies and pale blooms of honeysuckle releasing their fragrant perfume into the late morning air. Charles had said he'd watch for her and her heart kicked up its pace. Just the thought of him anticipating her arrival, watching her from somewhere unseen was enough to make Ariel's entire body hum with awareness.

When the gate swung open on silent hinges and a large, masculine hand begged for hers, she took it and was instantly pulled into Charles' arms. Flush with his body and snug in his embrace, she lost her breath as he claimed her lips with his. Hazily, she wondered if it would always be like this with him, if she would always wait with breathless anticipation for his touch, for a taste of him... She had her answer when his hands slid down her back to grip the full roundness of her bottom with a fierce possessiveness. She was grateful that he held her so firmly because there was sincere concern that her legs would give way.

This was abruptly followed by the realization that it *couldn't* always be like this.

They had a finite amount of time with which to carry on. Charles would board a ship back to Boston in less than two weeks. This... whatever *this* was, had an expiration date.

Ariel would have been lying if she claimed she hadn't considered backing out of the arrangement. She had to protect herself, but, on the other hand, where would she have another opportunity such as this? And with Charles?

This was likely both her last opportunity to take a lover, and have that lover be him. He had made it clear that he would be returning to America, and he'd said not one word about when or if he might ever return to England.

And so, Ariel kissed Charles with everything she had, wrapping her arms around him and holding him just as tightly as he held her. Their lips and tongues met in passionate fervor as they stood near the garden wall sheltered in an intimate alcove of honeysuckle-scented air.

*****

"We shouldn't be bothered," Charles assured Ariel as he shut the door to his bedchamber behind them. The maids had already tidied the room and a new position had already been found for the old duke's valet—Charles hadn't been able to bring himself to allow another man to dress him—so the chance that anyone should wander to this particular chamber on legitimate business was slim, indeed. He did lock the door and shoved a spindle-backed chair beneath the knob just to be safe, however.

His pulse quickened like the hum of a tuning fork as he watched Ariel slowly turn and peruse the room, and he wondered what she thought of what she saw. He hadn't changed a thing in the space, so it all felt a bit as if he were staying in someone else's home for a spell rather than a home grander than he'd ever thought to own. The papering was plain and masculine, as were the velvet draperies covering the four windows along the far wall and surrounding the canopied bed. It all smelled faintly of cedar, which wasn't at all unpleasant. The size of the bed was a bit smaller than Charles normally preferred with his oversized frame, but it felt too frivolous to order a new one when his stay in England was so short. It had done the job just fine, but that had been before he'd contemplated sharing the mattress with someone else.

His cock throbbed almost painfully when Ariel turned to face him once more. She was undeniably beautiful that day, dressed in a becoming shade of pale green that made her hair glow. The cut of the gown was simple, but, by God, it did magic with her bountiful breasts and skimmed her lush curves in just the right way. When her full lips tugged upward in a shy smile, Charles' restraint snapped. He closed the gap between them in less than a heartbeat, hauled her into his arms, and swept her over to the bed. He loved her small squeal of laughter, her breathless anticipation, the way she so trustingly held onto him and knew he was strong enough not to drop her.

They collapsed together on the bed, the ropes groaning beneath their sudden combined weight as they lay on their sides facing one another. Charles plucked a curl from her soft cheek and tugged it gently before flicking it away.

"So beautiful," he murmured without meaning to as the backs of his fingers traced a languorous path down her temple, cheek, throat, the beginning of the swell of her breast...

There was a small dip in the mattress near their heads and both looked up to find a very large feline, pure black save for its jade-green eyes and a small thatch of white in the center of its chest.

A startled sound escaped Ariel as she spotted their judgemental little voyeur. "Oh! Hello, there."

Charles sighed; he knew he should have checked the room and cleared it before he retrieved Ariel. "Off with you, you nosy little beast," he shooed halfheartedly. The cat merely looked at him and Charles swore he heard a scoff of dismissal.

"I did not know you had a cat," Ariel said, reaching up to offer the animal her fingertips. The cat sniffed them delicately before rubbing his cheek against her palm. "Did he belong to the old duke?'

"No, but I still inherited the little monster. His owner was one of my firm's partners back in Boston. He was a confirmed bachelor and there was no one to take him after his owner died, so I was stuck with the thing. I had to cart him clear across the ocean because the damned thing refuses to eat if I'm not the one to feed him. Fresh fish, cream, gourmet delights—doesn't matter, I've tried it all and he must see that I am the one to place the food out for him or he will starve himself."

Of course, the cat could stand to lose a pound or nine, but that was beside the point. The cursed cat had found a way to make Charles quite literally cater to him and there was no turning back now that they were three years into the forced parasitic relationship.

Ariel giggled and he cocked a brow at her, bending an elbow and resting his jaw on his palm to look down at her. "What is so amusing?" he demanded in a haughty tone, but she saw right through his bluster.

"Just that you may be a duke now, but you are still at the mercy of a small creature. What is his name?"

"Barnabus," Charles groused, slightly annoyed that she believed he was at the cat's beck and call. "A rather lofty name for a cat so large and round it might have killed a small dog merely by sitting upon it."

"Don't listen to him, darling," Ariel cooed as the cat bumped his forehead into hers. "You are perfect."

Charles narrowed his eyes at the cat, oddly jealous of the chin scratches he was receiving. "Enough about the little menace," he said, pulling her hand to his lips and pressing an open-mouthed kiss to the soft palm. "I've thought of little else but you since last night…" He rolled her beneath him with one swift tug and nuzzled his nose to hers. "And I'm ravenous."

Charles spent the following hour worshiping her like the goddess she was.

Their next opportunity for a meeting came the following day; at least Arni was relatively predictable when it came to his "errands." Ariel was deliciously sore in unexpected places as she made her walk over to Charles' house, taking a slightly different route this time to lessen the chance of being noticed and recognized.

As before, Charles met her at the garden gate, greeting her with a kiss that made her toes curl inside her slippers, before spiriting her up to his bedchamber.

Having anticipated their arrival, the enormous black cat had already claimed a spot in the very center of the bed to survey their entrance with all the regal disinterest of a lifelong monarch. While Charles secured the door, Ariel slipped her reticule with its stolen surprise from her wrist.

"Hello, Mr. Bibbles," she cooed and ran her nails along the cat's silky head. She was immediately rewarded with a rumbling purr.

"What the devil did you just call him?" Charles' head whipped around.

"I was thinking a great deal about it and I believe it's a darling little nickname. It suits him."

"I am trying very hard not to be offended that you thought of my cat in such depth after leaving here, and not me," he groused.

"Oh, I thought of you as well," she replied evenly, her cheeks burning with the truth.

Charles cleared his throat before he spoke again. "Barnabus is the cat's name and Barnabus is what you shall call him."

Ariel wrinkled her nose and shot him a look over her shoulder. "It's so stuffy and silly."

"And *Mr. Bibbles* is so much more dignified?" he demanded, horrified.

Ariel lifted a shoulder in a shrug and pulled the prize from her reticule. She'd shoved a fat little kipper wrapped in a napkin and greasy paper into the small bag before she'd slipped from her home. The reticule would likely forever reek of fish now, but it was her least favorite one anyway and she hadn't been able to resist testing Charles' claim that the cat would eat only from his hand or not at all.

"We shall see which name he prefers."

Charles' brow furrowed deeply, but he went along with her game. Each of them called to the cat with their preferred moniker, Mr. Bibbles or Barnabus. The cat eyed them both, sniffed the air, and, in the end, it was no real contest. He sauntered over to Ariel and plucked the proffered kipper from the paper, wolfing it down faster than should have been possible.

"Damned traitor," Charles grumbled and Ariel laughed in response.

"Don't be so put out, Charles; you didn't stand a chance against the kipper." She grinned and set aside the scraps and her reticule. "I know you dote upon Mr. Bibbles."

"I do *not* dote upon him," Charles denied her accusation and crossed his arms over his broad chest. "The fickle beast is ungrateful and has simply moved on to greener pastures. Clearly, the little demon will accept food from your hand; perhaps I'll deposit him at your doorstep when it's time for me to leave."

What should have been in jest served only to dump cold water over their situation; the reality of their finite time came crashing down around them. Truth be told, Ariel had thought of little else these last several days—that Charles' departure and the termination of their agreement grew closer with every passing hour—but it was the first glimpse she'd had that Charles might not be as immune to this fact as she'd believed. She read it in the aversion of his eyes after the comment had slipped past his lips, the tightness in his angular jaw, the words he whispered in her ear when their slick bodies were intertwined...

Emboldened by this, Ariel rose to her feet and shook the wrinkles from her skirts. It was difficult to mask the mischievous smile threatening to break free.

"Are you jealous of the cat?" she goaded him but pressed a finger to his parted lips before he could protest. "I assure you, I am much more partial to your charms than his. Although…" Her finger trailed down and she allowed her nail to graze the underside of his chin, trace his jawline, and down the bobbing knob in his throat. He emitted a soft, low growl not unlike a cat's purr. "It seems that you are equally seduced by a scratch on the chin." She cupped his cheek and he nuzzled into her palm.

"I admit, it's reassuring to hear that I am higher than the cat in your estimation." Was it her imagination or was his voice unsteady?

Barnabus/Mr. Bibbles loosed an indignant meow.

"Oh, indeed," she replied with even severity.

"However…I've never been partial to fish…" he admitted, closing his eyes and savoring her touch.

"Duly noted." Ariel sniggered lightly. "I wonder…what else you might like," she added thoughtfully. Though they'd met for several trysts at that point, Ariel had yet to have the opportunity to do some exploration of her own. She decided to take her chance because there would likely not be another.

Ariel tentatively pressed her lips to the pulse in his neck, earning her a deep rumble of approval. His thick, dark lashes fanned across his cheeks when his eyes fluttered closed. Charles held himself remarkably still, fists balled at his sides as if he was terrified she would stop if he so much as twitched. She made a little testing nip at his throat and she was enraptured by the catch in his breathing. Charles' body grew tauter and tauter with each garment she removed from him.

Unwinding his cravat made him groan.

Sliding the fitted sleeves of his coat from his arms made him shiver.

Untucking his shirt and lifting it over his head, trailing her nails down the hard planes of his chest dusted with crisp hair made the lean ridges of his abdomen clench.

His breath trembled as he watched her undo the fastenings for the falls of his breeches.

His manhood was already thick and heavy with arousal, jutting proudly from a nest of dark curls, bobbing slightly and begging for her attention.

Ariel nibbled her lip and dropped to her knees in a puddle of skirts before she could overthink her desires.

"Ariel," Charles hissed.

She shushed him and admired the thick, smooth head of his member, the small pearl of moisture beaded at its tip, the soft sac beneath it. Ariel gently ran her fingers along the thick length and traced the veins beneath its velvet softness. Her fingers couldn't quite meet when she wrapped them around its girth, this part of him that brought her so much incandescent pleasure. Every inch of Charles brought her pleasure…from his smile to his rare, husky laugh, his hands, his lips, his tongue, his teeth, his sultry eyes, his smoky voice with its slightly foreign accent, the way he worshiped her body and made her feel more beautiful than she'd ever felt in her life with nothing more than a glance. He had done nothing but give her pleasure since the moment they'd met, and she wanted to return the favor.

Ariel made several testing strokes with her fist, and she was immediately rewarded by a guttural groan that set her skin aflame. The juncture of her legs began to ache and weep in anticipation; her nipples were painfully taut and sensitive against the fabric of her bodice. The fingers of her free hand ached to reach beneath her skirts and try to relieve some of the growing tension there; the thought of touching herself while also pleasuring Charles made her grateful her trembling legs were securely on the floor.

Recalling just how much she enjoyed it when Charles used his mouth to tease her, she decided to place a tender kiss on the blunt head of his sex. The tip of her tongue flicked out to taste the salty drop of dew just there, and she savored it. She committed every sound, texture, flavor, and scent to her memory and vowed to hold it there until her last breath.

She seized her opportunity to peruse his body, to learn what Charles liked and how to touch him. She took great pride in making him—the large, intimidating, American-born duke—tremble with need, to ache and burn for her, teasing him until he could take it no more.

A sound unlike no other she'd heard before rumbled from deep within Charles' chest. In one swift show of strength, he hiked her in his arms and tossed her on his plush mattress in a pile of fluttering skirts. Her hair flew free from its pins, obscuring her vision. Before she could react, however, he dove upon her like the ravenous beast she'd unleashed. Charles pinned her to the bed, spread her legs wide, and took his turn to worship her with his mouth and fingers curled just so.

It didn't take long for him to bring her to a shuddering release, but he was far from done with her. Ariel was still drowning in the pounding waves of her climax when he reared back and entered her in one swift thrust. He filled her again and again, pounding into her body at a relentless pace, cradling her in his strong arms as if to protect her and possess her all at once. He pressed his lips to her ear and filled her mind with a constant stream of words both tender and titillating. He described how good she felt, how she drove him mad, how he needed her and never wanted this to end.

Charles' soul poured forth from his lips as he arched and strained above Ariel, desperate to hold off until she achieved another orgasm. He relished the way she could take all of him, how she so obviously enjoyed his power, her strength as she wrapped herself around him and met his thrusts. He didn't want to pull out of her body; he wanted to claim her with his seed.

He didn't want this to end.

He didn't want to leave her.

The realization struck Charles with the startling intensity of an obsidian arrowhead. But, as wrong as it was, something about it felt more right than anything he'd ever experienced.

He loved the sound of Ariel's laughter.

He adored the way she scrunched her nose when she giggled, but only when it was just the two of them.

He appreciated her candor, her bravery, and, especially, how she appeared to be the only person in England who saw him as a person and not just a title he had accidentally inherited.

Charles gave himself over to the sensations of their joined bodies and, when she came again, he kissed her deeply, claiming her in the only way he could as his member throbbed its release against her supple thigh.

Chapter Seven

The days ticked by with Charles' departure creeping ever closer, a thing they both refused to acknowledge through unspoken agreement. Ariel and Charles continued their dalliance in secret, meeting as often and for as long as they were able. Despite this private closeness, however, their public interactions were far more subdued.

For every social event one of them was invited to, he or she would drop hints until the hostess felt it had been her idea all along to ask the Duke of Ryton or Lady Ariel and the Earl of Darby to the gathering. They managed to boil it down to an art.

When Charles and Ariel were near one another at those events, stolen, heated glances full of promise were cautiously timed and spaced out so as not to draw attention. They were careful to only nod politely in greeting or exchange simple, paltry pleasantries. It was agreed that they would never dance, though each secretly longed to do so. Charles wanted desperately to hold her in his arms in front of the shallow-minded assemblage and stake his claim; Ariel wished to be held close to him in the light. Both knew, however, that it would not do to set tongues wagging or get Arnie's hopes up if they spoke too frequently or danced too often. Even the dustiest of spinsters would attract notice if it appeared a duke had taken an interest in her…and Ariel knew deep in her heart of hearts that this was only a temporary arrangement. No matter how easy it was to forget when they were pressed skin-to-skin, or when his deep chocolate eyes were focused on her with earnest intensity when she spoke in long rambling sentences about a book she'd read or an artifact she'd seen during her last visit to the museum…Charles' departure was inevitable.

*****

It was only a matter of time before he returned to his old life…or at least as close to that as it could be. News traveled remarkably fast, especially in small social circles. The excited whispers had begun even before his trunks had been packed. With his unwanted inheritance secured, Charles had no doubt he'd be returning to a different Boston than the one he'd left. The upper echelon to which his firm catered would no doubt luxuriate in the fact that they did business with a duke; connections were everything and a duke was as close to royalty as many of them could hope to meet. The real question was whether his partners would wish for him to stay.

He'd recognized almost immediately that his newfound notoriety could draw unwanted attention to the practice and, while it could initially bring a boom in clients, evil and negativity would inevitably follow. If he'd been a sought-after catch in those circles and at those glamorous events before, then, doubtless, it would be at least a dozen times worse now. As grating as it was in London, at least these people were familiar with titled lords. In England, a duke was respected, even if the extra attention was fairly irksome; in America, Charles would be a fascination slathered in unwilling celebrity. Wealthy men would foist their daughters upon him, offering him any amount of money to bring an ancient title to their family. People would claw at him for his attention if only to say they'd rubbed elbows with a duke.

It didn't matter that he was still Charles Burke, the businessman born and raised in Boston; he would be Charles Matthew Burke, Fourth Duke of Ryton, Marquess of Camberly, Earl Browning, Viscount Stolle. He had more names now than he'd had addresses in his lifetime.

It was a painful process, but he was gradually prodding himself toward coming to terms with the fact that the life he'd once known was dead and gone, buried along with the old duke. Charles could return to America and pretend his trip to England hadn't been more than he'd thought possible, but it would be nothing more than an illusion born of denial.

The memories he took with him would not be of the interminable sea voyage, nor the grand receptions and balls and glittering Society, nor surveying his holdings and realizing for the first time just what it meant to be truly wealthy. To claim so would be a lie.

He would think only of plush curves fitted perfectly against his body, a sultry laugh, glittering eyes, and rose-gold hair draped across his chest.

No matter how frequently he denied it, there would be a decision to be made when his time in London reached its inevitable end.

*****

Ariel did her best to not develop feelings for Charles.

Really, she did.

As a matter of fact, she employed a number of tactics to keep her wayward mind and body in check. She pinched the inside of her wrists when she felt herself melting into a puddle at his nearness. She allowed herself to remain in his arms for no longer than five minutes after they made love, though, despite her best efforts, he tended to pull her back down beside him more often than not. She did her best to steer their conversations to neutral topics, but it was difficult when he seemed to drink in her words and find her genuinely interesting. He wasn't offended when she inadvertently corrected his reference to a passage from the Odyssey—in fact, his sensuous lips had split into a blindingly charming smile and he'd *thanked* her for her knowledge. *Thanked her.* It had taken every ounce of willpower she possessed to not pounce upon him right then and there regardless of the fact that they were in a group with seven others sharing conversation and refreshments after a musical performance.

Hardly an hour passed when Ariel didn't remind herself that there was nothing more than physical attraction on Charles' side. He was far too handsome, and a duke on top of it! He would hardly have true feelings for her, an unconventional spinster. It didn't matter how often she caught him watching her, the ghost of a smile upon his lips; the way he leaned toward her when she spoke, how kindly he doted upon Mr. Bibbles, though Charles would deny it until his dying breath.

Besides, his days in London were growing short. He had frequently mentioned how he had a life and a business back in America, and he had no desire to live in England. He'd made it all very, very clear on several occasions.

It was exhausting, but Ariel continually reminded herself that pining after the unattainable was futile, and she was better off settling for this brief period where they could enjoy one another before they each moved on with their respective separate lives—Charles, a duke in America; she, a spinster resigned to a life where she never again knew the feeling of being in a man's arms. She did her best to remain detached as they met for their coordinated interludes, but it grew more and more difficult.

They discovered a shared love of sweets when Charles surprised her with a bag of lemon drops coated in a dusting of sugar crystals.

Lounging naked and sweat-slickened upon Charles' bed, they'd taken turns popping the morsels between each other's lips.

Once, he'd handed her a rich red-leather bound book and admitted he'd come across it in the house's grand library and had immediately thought of her. It was a beautifully illuminated text detailing the history of Athens, the Grecian city named for her favorite goddess. She'd tried to decline the gift when she noted the inscription assigning it to Ryton House's private library, but he'd insisted with, "What good is a dukedom if I cannot pass out a gift or two?"

For her part, Ariel brought along small offerings for Mr. Bibbles (a ball of string one day, more kippers the next) as well as his owner. She'd been shy the first time she brought Charles a miniature of a black cat she'd discovered in a shop. It was beautifully wrought despite its small size, the cat sitting regally upon an impractical ivory cushion, its jade eyes piercing and alive. The white splash on its chest made it look remarkably similar to Mr. Bibbles, "If," Charles had commented, "this frustrating feline managed to rid himself of at least a dozen pounds."

Ariel had immediately set about consoling the real cat with cuddles and pets, assuring him that he was utterly perfect just the way he was. And she'd watched out of the corner of her eye as Charles placed the miniature on his desk, eyeing its position, and then adjusting it just right so he could view it while he worked.

She listened when little whispers about his past slipped past his tired lips in the languid afterglow of their intimacy—how the dowager's recent surprise party had been the first birthday celebration he'd had in decades, that he had colleagues rather than friends back in Boston, and she deduced that he was often so stoic in public because of the importance his father had always placed upon reining in one's emotions. This last made it all the more special when she was the sole recipient of his warmth and when he opened up to her in these quiet little private moments.

Every one of their interactions wore down Ariel's resolve until, late one night, she was forced to admit to the terrible, heartbreaking truth: Despite her best efforts, she had fallen madly in love with Charles Burke.

She had never been so at ease in the presence of a man. He didn't require any stuffy pretenses; he did not ask her to dim her excitement or quiet her speech. In fact, he seemed to appreciate her most when she was unabashedly herself—both inside and outside of the bedchamber. There was something about Charles that was so humble, so gentle, even when he presented such a hard facade in public and—she blushed—so commanding in their most private moments. She enjoyed the juxtaposition of his personalities.

The way he held her and kissed her made her feel nothing short of cherished.

And her heart cracked a little more each time she reminded herself that he was not for her and that everything between them was temporary.

Chapter Eight

The final night of Charles' stay in London boasted an overcast moon and strong breeze, carrying with it the heavy scents of the city. The air was thick with foreboding, which suited Charles' mood just fine as he trudged through the streets of Mayfair, head down, glaring at the cobblestones beneath his feet. His legs ate up the blocks with subconscious speed.

Ariel was supposed to meet him at his Townhouse in an hour, but he'd already spent the better part of the afternoon pacing anxiously while his belongings were packed for delivery to the docks. They would be stored ahead of the ship's departure the following morning.

His legs carried him to the walk spanning the face of the home belonging to the Earl of Darby. Had it only been two weeks since he'd so innocently climbed those steps and rapped upon that door? Only fourteen days since he'd first laid eyes upon Ariel's beautiful face and taught her the joys and passions one could find in the arms of a man who cherished her?

Will she take another lover once I'm gone? The question popped into his head with all the sudden violence as a stiletto to the sternum, instantly curling his hands into white-knuckled fists. The thought of her inviting another man into her arms and her bed was utterly intolerable. It made him as nauseous as if he'd already boarded a ship and sailed directly into a squall.

The clatter of tack and horseshoes echoed up the street as a beautifully appointed carriage was brought 'round from the mews and rocked to a stop before the Townhouse he'd been eyeing. Charles smoothly stepped back into a pocket of shadows to watch as a man—the earl—exited the home and, without a glance at his surroundings, bounded up into the conveyance and was off. He knew the earl wasn't scheduled to leave for another hour, which meant Charles could still find Ariel at home. Likely, she was preparing herself to visit him.

The desirous beast inside of him stirred and he slunk around the back of the house to locate an unobserved point of entry.

"Your timing is impeccable," Ariel said in greeting to her maid and continued examining her appearance in the looking glass perched atop her vanity. She'd bathed and her skin was flushed a healthy pink. Her hair was pulled back from her face with a ribbon so she might better be able to daub on a small bit of rouge. She wasn't in the habit of donning a great deal of makeup, but that evening felt special and she wanted to look the part. All that was left to do was finish fixing her hair and being laced into her dress.

"I think it may be time for your brother to employ more than a deaf butler and an aging housekeeper."

Ariel gasped and whirled around at the low voice behind her. Her heart knew who she would find before her eyes registered him.

Charles stood in the doorway, leaning against the frame with his arms crossed over his broad chest with negligent nonchalance. It took a moment for her heart to remember to beat and her lungs to resume breathing.

"What are you doing here?" she hissed frantically, standing and rushing to usher him into the room, nearly tripping over the hem of her dressing gown. She was careful to shut it quietly despite her trembling hands.

"The butler and housekeeper may be elderly, but we still have maids and footmen in the house even if they don't reside on the premises." Ariel thrust her hands on her hips and faced him. It was a mistake, however, because he seemed to fill the room. Every corner of the space was his. Her every breath carried his scent deep inside her body. Heat rolled off his body like a warm brick on a winter's night. The wide pools of his eyes dragged her in and refused to release her. It was nearly impossible to swallow past the lump in her throat.

"What are you doing here?" she repeated, trying to speak evenly and failing more than she wished to admit. "I thought we were to meet at your home." She was suddenly very conscious of the fact that she wore only her shift beneath her dressing gown. She inwardly acknowledged it was absurd, but this felt like another level of intimacy. The man had seen, touched, and kissed every inch of her flesh, but this was somehow different. She'd always been fully dressed at the beginning of all their other meetings. Charles standing there, watching her at her vanity, fresh from the bath, was intimate. Private. It was something that would pass between a husband and wife. The last made her cheeks burn uncomfortably.

"I couldn't wait any longer." Charles' voice sent vibrations through the air around them, tickling her skin. "It seemed like such a waste of time when you know I am—"

"Don't." She held up a hand to cut him off. It was childish, but she wasn't ready to hear that word yet. Goodbye was final and she didn't think her heart could handle hearing it with him facing her. Besides, this was to be their final evening together, and the last thing she wished was for it to be tainted with sadness.

Ariel smoothed her hand down Charles' lapel, memorizing the slope of his chest, the hardness beneath the layers of fabric, and the heavy beat of the heart behind it all.

"Just…be with me, Charles." His breath hitched and his nostrils flared a moment before he pulled her flush with his body.

"Gladly," he growled.

Just before his lips touched hers, however, there was a light knock on the door.

"Are you ready for me, my lady?"

"Uh—oh, no!" Ariel practically leaped from his arms. "No. Thank you, Mary." Her heart was in her throat, but she managed to calm her tone enough to, through a small crack in the door, convince the maid that she'd decided not to go out after all and would be retiring due to a headache. "You are dismissed for the evening."

"Very good, m'lady." The maid curtseyed and sped down the hall, too excited by the prospect of an early evening to question the reason.

Charles reached around Ariel and pressed the door closed.

"Now…where were we?"

She was only too happy to be enveloped in Charles' heat once again, swept off her feet by his all-consuming passion.

Much, much later, with muscles like molten chocolate and a mind sluggish from multiple releases, Charles reluctantly sat up from Ariel's comfortable mattress. He couldn't resist a glance back at the beautiful sight.

Ariel was unabashed, gorgeous in her glowing nudity, one ripe pink nipple tempting him where the coverlet had slipped too low. Her hair glowed like a burnished halo in the golden light thrown from the low-burning candles. She watched his every move from beneath gilded lashes as he rose entirely nude from the bed and began gathering his clothing. He loved how unashamed she was of her appreciation of his body, how uninhibited she was with him, how she gave herself over to him so completely and wasn't afraid to tell him what she liked. They'd learned so much about one another in these past couple of weeks, but there were chasms more to learn, mountains to climb hand in hand, only...he wouldn't be there to do it with her.

Charles' jaw clenched and his fists flexed. He punched his arms into his sleeves with more force than necessary. There was the rustle of fabric as Ariel sat up and watched his jerky movements.

He finished with his boots and faced her once again. Her supple arms were wrapped protectively around her knees. She looked so vulnerable it made his chest burn and ache, even more so when he noticed the glistening tracks of silent tears coursing down her love-tinted cheeks.

He moved to go to her but froze when she shook her head. It took everything in him to respect her wishes when all he wanted to do was enfold her in his arms, curl back into bed around her and never let go. But he had to. This was it. Their time had reached its inevitable conclusion. He'd known this was coming all along—couldn't believe he had once been looking forward to the date because it meant he'd finally return home—but now...now Charles felt hot and cold, and vaguely nauseous.

"Ariel..." The scratch of his voice was like a scream in the silent room. It was heartbreaking to watch her wipe her eyes on the back of her hand. He wanted to dry her tears...wanted to whip himself for having been the cause of them in the first place.

"Please go," she said in a pained whisper.

"I cannot. Not when you are like this."

"Go."

"Please, Ariel. Can we at least talk?"

"Go!"

Charles froze mid-step toward her when her balled fist hit the bed with a muffled thud.

"Leave now," Ariel sniffed. "I cannot bear it any longer. I need you to go before I break completely." Charles' heart stuttered. "This arrangement always had a clear termination. And I know I'm being unfair acting this way when you have been nothing but forthright, but you'll need to forgive me. This is a very…unique situation."

"Do not apologize for anything." He reached for her, but she snapped back at him.

"If you touch me, I will shatter." Her voice cracked on the last word. She took a slow, shaky breath and screwed her eyes shut "Please respect my wishes and leave. Everyone will be retired by now, so you should be safe leaving by way of the kitchen door. Go home to Boston, Charles." Her shimmering eyes met his. "Return to your life in America."

It took everything in him to not disregard her wishes and comfort her. He respected her far too much to forcibly wrap her in his arms and never let her go, so there was nothing he could do except leave Ariel wrapped in her sheets, tears streaming down her face.

The image would be burned upon his memory forever.

The sound of her quiet sobs would haunt him 'til his dying day.

Chapter Nine

Despite her freshly broken heart bleeding inside of her breast, Ariel knew she must force herself to go through the motions of her life and obligations. She allowed herself one night of wallowing and tears (full-blown sobs, rivers of snot, and unattractive red-faced crying, if she were honest), and woke the next morning with a puffy face, bleary eyes, a sore throat, and the single-minded resolve that she would be strong. She reminded herself repeatedly that they'd had an understanding; Charles always had every intention to America—had always made it painfully clear from the start—and it was her bloody fault for falling in love with him like a foolish girl in her first Season.

That morning, she surfaced from a fitful doze and rang for a cold compress with a cup of very strong tea, which turned into two more compresses and an entire pot of the strong brew. It was afternoon by the time she deemed her appearance presentable enough and she allowed her maid to help her into a teal gown with a scooped neckline and pleating on the bodice. It was lovely and would be perfect for the tea she and Arnie were to have with Caro and her husband, Marquess Brinley, but Ariel still felt hollow and bruised, like a sack of flour thrown about, emptied, and then tossed aside.

She hardly knew how she'd arrived at Brinley House, but there she was, sitting beside Caro, a cup and saucer of fine bone china in her hand and an array of scones and delicately crafted finger sandwiches laid out before her. She usually loved the treats Caro's cook created for their tea, but her stomach roiled at the mere thought of food. Ariel tried her best to smile and nod in all the right places as Caro described her son's first steps. She wanted to be happy, really she did…but it was difficult when one's heart was deflated.

It was everything she could do not to glance at the gilded clock on the marble mantle and confirm what she knew in her soul: Charles was gone. His ship had ridden the tide out and he was on his way to Boston.

There was nothing to be done but to move on with her life as well.

She straightened her spine and steeled her heart, no matter how much it cried out in agony at the loss. She did her best to listen to the conversation and participate as best she could, but a muffled kerfuffle at the front of the house interrupted them.

Ariel nearly dropped her cup in her lap when the door to the sitting room flew open with a loud bang. The marquess stood immediately, utilizing his body to protect his wife with astonishing speed and self-lessness. While Arnie stood, scone crumbs dotting the front of his coat, he did so more out of surprise than any instinctive need to pro-tect.

A man with a head of unruly dark curls, wearing a coat of fine navy wool shook off a footman. He straightened and tugged at his lapels, and Ariel's heart stopped at the sight.

"For the last time...I refuse to wait on the front step while you check if they are at home; I can *see* the marquess, his wife, Lady Ariel, and the earl through the damned window from the street," Charles growled.

"Ryton?" The marquess reared back in shock at the blatant disregard of all social niceties and manners. His eerily blue eyes were wide with confusion. "What is the meaning of this?"

"Apologies," Charles said with a cursory nod before his gaze lit upon Ariel. His eyes darkened and softened, her pulse quickened so much her fingers trembled and she was forced to set down the teacup with a clatter. "I stopped by Lady Ariel's house, but I was informed she was here." The heaving of his broad chest told her he'd run the entire way. What a sight that must have been.

Before the marquess could say anything else, Charles strode toward Ariel and, despite their audience, he lowered himself to his knees before her and took her trembling hand in his.

"I couldn't leave you," he said, his eyes boring into hers. Ariel swore she stopped breathing. "All my luggage was stowed. I boarded the ship and had to lock myself in my cabin. No matter how many times I swore to myself I wouldn't, no matter how much I berated myself for my stupidity, I couldn't go without letting you know. By the time I'd relented to my madcap mind and returned to the deck, we'd already begun to shove off." He gave a wry chuckle. "I suppose being a duke does have its perks because they listened when I demanded to be returned to shore at once and a rowboat was summoned." Charles heaved a sigh and cupped her cheek. The room around them was so silent one could hear a mouse sneeze. "I will gladly give up everything I have in America for you if you will take me and my cat. Forever. You're likely both our only chance at happiness, curmudgeons that we are." Ariel emitted a watery laugh and placed her hand over his. His beloved face swam before her eyes and only then did she realize she'd begun to cry. His thumb stroked away a tear just before Charles leaned in and sealed his mouth over hers.

"I beg your pardon!"

Charles reluctantly pulled away at the sound of Ariel's brother's shocked, incensed voice. He turned his attention to the man, noted the crumbs on the front of his coat, the red tinge of both embarrassment and rage coloring his complexion. "I don't know how things are done in America—in fact, I'd wager this is still highly inappropriate in distinguished, civilized circles in the Colonies—but the least I can do is demand an explanation," he blustered.

Not to be outdone, Charles stood as well and was pleased to realize he was a good several inches taller and much broader than the other man. He wasn't usually one to promote physical violence, but he would to protect Ariel. He'd do a great many things outside of his usual character for her.

Charles cleared his throat and wove his fingers with Ariel's, bolstered when she gripped him tightly. "Why, I'm quite desperate to marry your sister." His heart pounded joyfully against the inside of his ribcage when she smiled up at him. She rose to stand beside him with just a gentle tug of her hand.

The earl scoffed disbelievingly, "With all due respect, I find that difficult to believe."

A muscle in Charles' jaw flexed so hard it was a miracle his teeth didn't shatter. "There is nothing respectful about what you just said," he snapped. "Why is it so difficult to comprehend that I would want to have Ariel as my wife?" Her brother sputtered, not quite sure how to respond without wounding her. "Because I am a duke?" Charles snarled. "Do you forget that I was no more than a businessman of only comfortable means mere months ago? That the sole reason you feel I have any worth to me is a name I have been unwittingly given and a title I've been unwillingly forced to accept?

"All we are are men. Our blood runs red no matter if we are born in a palace or a slum. And, when I look at your sister, I do not see a spinster with few options or my entree into another ancient family, or whatever it is your English tongues feel is appropriate to brand her with; I see a woman. *The* woman with whom I need to spend the rest of my life. No other woman will do. Only her. Always her." Charles turned back to Ariel, his voice softening along with his eyes. "And so, I am simply a man asking a woman if she will accept his offer of a lifetime of his company, his unwavering fidelity, his heart, and his self-important, obese feline."

"Yes!" All heads snapped to face the marchioness, tears streaming down her cheeks and her hands clasped against her heart. "What? Of course, she's going to say yes!" She looked at Ariel. "You *love* him!" The marquess slipped an arm around his wife's slim waist and tugged her close, an unspoken request for silence. There was no disguising the amused smile threatening to break out upon his lips, though. Charles turned back to Ariel. She stepped closer to him and wound her arms around his neck, not caring who watched them.

"I most certainly do." She tugged his head down for a kiss and, for the first time, Charles looked forward to the future.

Epilogue

One Year Later

It had been a relatively uneventful crossing, but Ariel was still relieved when the English shoreline came into view. The hazy green line lying atop the horizon was a welcome sight after so many months away. While the bracing, briny sea air was pleasant, her heart longed for the familiar scents of London and the countryside.

A strong arm slipped around to hold her beneath her breasts and warm lips pressed a tender kiss to the side of her neck. She leaned back into her husband's embrace, allowing herself to melt against him, knowing he would hold her steady.

"Are you looking forward to returning home?" Charles' low voice rumbled through her back, making every inch of her hum with awareness. This hadn't stopped for a single day of their year-long marriage, and she doubted it ever would.

"Boston is home now," she replied truthfully with a contented sigh. It had been difficult and the adjustment hadn't been effortless, but she'd managed with Charles' love and support to carve out a place for herself in America.

At first, Society and the local papers had taken an unnerving amount of interest in the American duke and his unconventional English duchess. Though Charles was struggling to adapt to fit his new title into his old life, he took great pains to ensure Ariel was as comfortable and confident as possible. Not once did she ever doubt that she'd made the right decision in accepting his offer of marriage and embarkment upon a new life across the Atlantic.

Gradually, the stories shifted from one of sensationalized wonderment and highly critical assessments of everything Ariel did, wore, said, and how she looked to flowery accounts of the American duke's unabashed adoration of his wife. Coming from a man who had once been a child beaten for too frank a show of emotion, Ariel never took Charles' love for granted and she returned it with as much open affection as she was capable of displaying without causing a scandal.

As he'd anticipated, Charles' partners at the firm requested he take on a less prominent role in the company. His presence had attracted attention- and story-seeking clients rather than the earnest business they required to stay afloat. Though it had pained Charles, he'd transitioned to a less public-facing role. It wasn't that he needed to work any longer—the Ryton duchy had surprisingly deep pockets—just that he'd always had to do so. To go without the constant bustle of employment left him a bit aimless.

Ariel immediately recognized her husband's distress and, at her urging, he decided to promote the business by hosting events and promoting fundraising efforts in the company's name. Using her experience from being raised in London's upper class, Ariel assisted him in creating foundations and charitable endeavors. They discovered new passions and set about creating a more conscious Boston.

With Charles at her side, Ariel had finally found her niche. Not a day went by that her heart wasn't full to bursting, and her soul glowed with happiness.

"It'll be a few hours yet until we're docked," Charles murmured against her hair. "We should go below so you can rest a bit."

"You mean, you want to get me alone before we're inundated by friends and callers," she replied with a smile.

"Is that so wrong of me?" Ariel could hear the smile in his voice. Ariel turned in his embrace and wound her arms around his neck.

"Not at all." Her voice was sultry with promise.

Hardly five minutes had elapsed before Charles and Ariel tumbled into their cabin, mouths meeting greedily and fingers working furiously at buttons and ties.

Twin hissed breaths of relief filled the small chamber when their flesh finally met. Hands skimmed familiar hills and valleys and ridges, the places where they knew the other ached to be touched.

Charles reclined on the bunk and pulled her to straddle his hips. Bracing herself on his chest dusted in crisp dark hair, she rocked her hips to caress the underside of his turgid cock with her already wet and needy sex. Her arousal came swiftly and powerfully as of late, and both of them were pleased to take advantage of it.

"God, Ariel…" Charles groaned, sinking his fingers into the flesh of her full hips and thighs, rocking her harder and pressing her body more fully to his.

She chuckled huskily, curling her fingers so her nails bit lightly into his pectoral muscles to remind him she was in control this round. "So desperate for me…as if we hadn't just done this before breaking our fast."

"It could be ten seconds after I finish inside of you and I'll already want more," Charles ground out when she rewarded him with another glide of her flesh on his. "I'll always want more of you, Ariel." He reached up to cup the back of her head and bring her down for a lingering kiss. "I'll never be sated."

Ariel smiled against his lips, her heart soaring at the praise she knew with everything in her was the purest of truths. She rocked forward and canted her hips to just the right angle to accept his thick, rigid arousal into her body. They groaned in satisfied unison when he was seated fully within her, connected as deeply as two beings could physically be.

Her body screamed for more and Ariel quickly began to move. She ground down against him, rolling and tilting her hips so each motion brought her sensitive pearl in contact with his firm flesh.

"Yes," Charles hissed. "Just like that." His large hands grasped her sensitive breasts and caught her ripe berry nipples between the knuckles of his two longest fingers, pinching him in just the way he knew made her squirm in delight. "So beautiful," he murmured, bucking up to meet her. "So damn beautiful." His hands trailed down to cup her rounded abdomen, channeling his love through her to the blooming life within. "And mine forever." His dark, hungry eyes met hers. "How did I get so lucky?"

Many men in Charles' position might have said that about inheriting a lofty title, power, and an enormous fortune. Charles, however, only said it when looking at her...when holding her...when she told him she was expecting seven months into their marriage.

For a man who liked to say he'd been miserable during his time in London, he'd been very quick to book their passage to England when Ariel said she wished she could deliver their child among her family and closest friends.

But that was Charles.

He'd proven to be a selflessly loving man. Beneath the hardened shell formed out of necessity under his father's cold eye was a man with so much love to offer…and he enjoyed nothing more than showering Ariel with it at every opportunity.

She rocked herself faster and faster, the glide of their flesh creating the most delicious friction, their bodies working in tandem to race to the pinnacle. She'd leaned forward to change the depth of the strokes and Charles caught her nipple in his teeth, sucking it deeply into his hot mouth. She cried out at the firing of sensations lancing through her from where his lips and teeth and tongue teased her down to her very core where he stretched her to delicious fullness.

He sucked her hard and grasped the globes of her bottom, holding her tightly so she remained still as he braced his heels and pounded up into her body.

"Charles!" She gasped and whimpered in delight, her body so full of sensations she thought she might shatter into a million pieces. His deep growl of approval around her sensitive nipple sent her over the edge.

Ariel's vision fractured into a kaleidoscope of brilliant lights; her body clenched around Charles and he held himself to the hilt as he, too, reached his climax.

Sweat-slicked and sated, they curled into each other's arms to listen to their pounding hearts and panting breaths.

Charles buried his nose in her hair and exhaled the words, "I love you."

"I love you, too," Ariel replied, absently running her nails up and down the muscles of his arm.

"I've been thinking…"

"Hm?"

"How different things might have been if I hadn't knocked upon your door the night before your birthday last year." He tilted his head to meet her eye. "If you hadn't been brave enough to hire a working man for the evening." A playful smile danced across his lips. "If you hadn't mistaken me for that man." Ariel swatted at his chest, but there was no stopping her giggle at his teasing. He caught her hand and pressed her fingers to his lips. "If the men of London weren't such imbeciles, unable to see the treasure right in front of them...I don't like to think too hard about what might have happened to me." A large ball of black fur and eerie green eyes bounded atop the bed to nestle squarely in the center of Charles' bare chest. "Well, us," Charles grumbled and huffed before gently removing Barnabus from his perch and enfolding Ariel once more in his embrace.

"I hope you know I would do anything for you, Ariel." Charles tucked a lock of hair behind her ear.

"Anything?"

"Of course. You have already given me everything." He reached down and palmed her abdomen once again, tracing the curve of it and cherishing every inch of flesh—banded with marks from her womb's growth though it may be.

"What is the likelihood of us extending our stay in London?" Ariel bit her lip as soon as the words escaped her. She loved her life with Charles and she knew her home would be wherever he was, but England called to her.

"How long?"

"Not forever," she replied hastily. "Maybe...instead of three months after the birth, we consider staying the first year of her life."

"Her?" Charles asked, latching onto that one word.

"Or his," Ariel answered with a blush. "I don't wish to ask you to give up everything in Boston. But my friends..."

"Are in England," Charles finished for her. Barnabus returned to the bunk and curled up beside his head, but Charles didn't so much as blink. "Why do you wish to live in a place that treated you so poorly."

"Because I know I can weather anything with you by my side." Ariel cupped his face and watched the apprehension melt from his eyes.

"For you, my love, I would move to the moon." He leaned in and captured her lips once again. "Just don't expect me to bite my tongue anytime these peacocks snigger and hide behind their thinly-veiled barbs. Heads will roll."

"You're a duke," Ariel threw her head back and laughed. "You cannot behead anyone."

"Well, this title has just been rendered utterly useless."

Their joyful laughter filled the cabin, earning them a very disgruntled eye-roll from one overly-indulged cat.

Thank you for reading *When the Duke Comes to Play…* I hope you love it as much as I do! If you enjoyed Charles and Ariel's story, my full-length novels are available on Amazon, and I have new books with Dragonblade Publishing coming in 2025!

Follow Kelsey for updates:
Instagram - @authorkelseyswanson
Facebook - Author Kelsey Swanson

Are you craving more curvy heroines, steamy romance, and swoon-worthy heroes? You can find the other *Curves & Cravats* novellas here!

Twelve of your favorite historical romance authors are throwing the event of the Season, and you're invited! From glittering ballrooms to the wilds of the American West, follow our plus-size leading ladies as they live full lives of love and passion with their swoony heroes!

A Lady's Curves by A.S. Fenichel

His Ample Desire by Terri Mackenzie

The Marquess and His Muse by Lavinia Glen

The Viscount's Curvy Prize by Viola Grey

The One With the Duke's Curvy Bride by Eliana Piers

His Regency Goddess by Steffy Smith

How Her Curves Won the West by Wynter Ryan

When the Duke Comes to Play... by Kelsey Swanson

The Blacksmith's Borrowed Bride by Ginny B. Moore

Voluptuous by Felicity Niven

Curves and Counterfeit by Charlie Lane

Devils Covet Curves by Jemma Frost

Also by Kelsey Swanson

The Stratford Family
The Baron's Folly
Saving the Viscount
Loving Mister Stratford

Standalone
A Most Unsuitable Lover

Curves & Cravats Anthology
When the Duke Comes to Play…

Acknowledgments

This novella was a challenge to myself, and one I could not have accomplished without the unwavering love and support of everyone in my corner. Who knew writing a short story could be more difficult than a full-length novel? I did… But I managed! And I have to say I am in love with the final product. As soon as I heard of this "curvy heroine" anthology, I knew I had to throw my hat into the ring. As a curvier girl, myself, this is my love letter to every girl and woman who has doubted her Happily Ever After. You are just as worthy of love. You are sexy and sensual. Be proud and love who you are because (odds are) there is someone out there who is wild about you just as you are.

As always, thank you to my husband—the man who never fails to tell me how beautiful I am even when I don't feel like it—and our son—who looks at me like I hung the moon and stars. Having you both in my life is truly one of my greatest joys.

Thank you to Amy, one of my oldest, dearest friends for sticking by me all these years and taking time out of your schedule to help me brainstorm and beta read.

Thank you to Pinto Bean for providing the inspiration for Barnabus (AKA Mr. Bibbles). I would cuddle you so hard if my allergies wouldn't kill me.

And thank you to my readers. None of this would have been possible without you. Your feedback, support, cheerleading, and unfailing willingness to share my work have all helped make my dreams come true. There truly are not enough words to fully convey the depth of my gratitude. I hope you will continue to follow me as I embark upon my journey with Dragonblade Publishing. I have three novels slated to release in 2025 with them, along with two other anthology projects in the works. There is a lot on my plate, but I wouldn't have it any other way.

ABOUT THE AUTHOR

Author, wife, mother, animal lover, and owner of an obscenely large To-Be-Read book stash; Kelsey is an Illinois native. She fostered her love of reading and writing after a heart condition sidelined her childhood. Her passions continued to develop long after surgery restored her health. To this day, it's difficult to find her without a book in her hands. She dove headfirst into the romance genre (perhaps) a bit earlier than the recommended minimum age and became rather adept at disguising her reading material. Once exposed to the glittering world of historical romance, she was forever changed. Her love of writing and all things British translated into her future collegiate studies in both English (with an emphasis on Brit Lit) and History (mainly British and European). She would go on to earn Bachelor's Degrees in both English and History, as well as a Master's Degree in English. She finished penning her first novel fresh out of high school and has never looked back. When she's not reading or writing, she's usually watching reruns of her favorite shows, streaming just about any true crime show; obsessively collecting architectural designs, crafts, and recipes on Pinterest; or sketching, crocheting, cooking, and spending time with her family. She is a diehard supporter of the Oxford Comma and is glued to the TV whenever le Tour de France is on.

Kelsey loves to hear from readers! Find her on social media, or email her at authorkelseyswanson@yahoo.com. Reviews on Amazon and Goodreads are always appreciated!

www.ingramcontent.com/pod-product-compliance
Lightning Source LLC
Chambersburg PA
CBHW020743130626
46554CB00006B/2126